Dear Reader,

Who can forget their first love? Or their first heartbreak?

In *Just For the Night,* Larissa Zahn reunites with both when she sees Jason Cantrell again. And all she wants is to get away. Enter Fate, always a wily trickster, in the form of a huge power outage. Suddenly, Larissa finds herself alone with Jason, trapped…for twenty-four hours!

This book was such fun to write because I got to spend a lot of time with two characters who are so perfect for each other, yet haven't got a clue. There's nothing like a little forced confinement (and a yummy jar of chocolate body paint) to stir up some sexy adventure!

If you're on the web, please drop by my website at www.tawnyweber.com and let me know what you think of Jason and Larissa's story. While you're there, check out my blog, vote for the hunk of the month or enter my current contest. I'd love to hear from you.

Tawny Weber

# Tawny Weber

## JUST FOR THE NIGHT

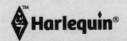

TORONTO NEW YORK LONDON
AMSTERDAM PARIS SYDNEY HAMBURG
STOCKHOLM ATHENS TOKYO MILAN MADRID
PRAGUE WARSAW BUDAPEST AUCKLAND

Recycling programs
for this product may
not exist in your area.

ISBN-13: 978-0-373-79616-8

JUST FOR THE NIGHT

Copyright © 2011 by Tawny Weber

This edition published by arrangement with Harlequin Books S.A.

For questions and comments about the quality of this book please contact us at Customer_eCare@Harlequin.ca.

www.Harlequin.com

**Printed in U.S.A.**

## ABOUT THE AUTHOR

Tawny Weber is usually found dreaming up stories in her California home, surrounded by dogs, cats and kids. When she's not writing hot, spicy stories for Harlequin Blaze, she's shopping for the perfect pair of shoes or scrapbooking happy memories. Come by and visit her on the web at www.tawnyweber.com.

## Books by Tawny Weber

### HARLEQUIN BLAZE

To get the inside scoop on Harlequin Blaze and its talented writers, be sure to check out blazeauthors.com.

Don't miss any of our special offers. Write to us at the following address for information on our newest releases.

Harlequin Reader Service
U.S.: 3010 Walden Ave., P.O. Box 1325, Buffalo, NY 14269
Canadian: P.O. Box 609, Fort Erie, Ont. L2A 5X3

To Beth Andrews, my best friend and awesome critique partner. Thank you for always being there, always seeing the heart of my stories and always cheering me on. I couldn't do it without you!

## 1

"FOR A GIRL WHO ISN'T about to get laid, you're spending an awful lot of time obsessing over your underwear choices."

"These are important decisions," Larissa Zahn insisted as she sifted through the multitude of fabrics and patterns in the satin-lined box. "My entire future could be riding on this."

"On the choice between lace and satin?" Chloe Carpenter, Larissa's oldest friend and current roommate asked with a laugh. "C'mon, 'Risa. Put your panties away and let's go see a movie."

"I don't have time for a movie tonight. I need to make sure I have the perfect selection of merchandise for the test display tomorrow. I want to show Cartright's team that my concept for Isn't It Romantic will fit perfectly in their hotel's mall." Larissa waved a hand at the myriad of merchandise strewn all over the living room.

Boxes of romance, she'd been calling them over the last eight months as she collected possible items to stock when she opened her store. She stared, wild-eyed, at the mess. At the moment, it seemed a little more like an obsession gone overboard.

"Haven't you picked out your perfect selection already?"

Chloe lifted a red binder over her head and waved it around, tabbed pages of lists, photos and sketches fluttering like little tattletale flags. "Like, four times at least?"

Looking at the notebook, Larissa gave Chloe a weak smile. She knew her friend was right. Once upon a time, her dream had been easy. Since she was a teenager, she'd dreamed of buying the cozy independent bookstore she worked in, of getting married to her true love and starting a family. But two years ago, that dream had fallen apart. So she'd rebuilt her dream. This one depended on her and nobody else.

She'd started by asking herself what she believed in enough to devote her business, her time and all of her attention to. The answer? Romance.

Despite a heart-bruising breakup, Larissa still believed in romance. But romance with rules. The kind that kept a girl from getting so caught up in the fluff she got hurt by the reality. So just for fun—and, yes, as a way to clarify her own set of romance rules—Larissa had started a blog two years ago. Quickly gaining in popularity, it had swiftly grown into a monthly newsletter which had also become a huge hit. At first it had been about all of the wonderful romance novels she loved, pointing out the strength of the heroines. But over the last year it'd expanded to include songs and movies, romantic getaways and recipes for breakfast in bed. All things romantic. Six months ago, her fun little column, *Larissa's Rules of Romance,* had been picked up as a monthly feature in a nationally syndicated magazine. Now, in addition to her column, she also answered romance questions and offered tidbits of advice to the entire country.

It'd been the perfect foundation to use to open a store. All things romantic, based on her rules, advice and observations. She'd carry books, movies and music, of course. But she'd have more. Everything a woman could want to bring more romance into her life. The only thing Larissa needed was a location.

Only now that the most amazing location was right there, a fingertip away, she wasn't sure she was ready for her pitch. She knew the display she set up was crucial to selling her idea, so it had to be perfect. But did she go old-fashioned romance or modern-day romance? Did she focus on her favorites—books, movies and music—or should she make the gifts and romantic mementos the centerpiece of her presentation?

"You look like your head is about to explode," Chloe pointed out with a worried look. "Maybe you're right. We should stay in tonight."

Larissa shrugged that off. She knew she looked like hell. Her shoulder-length curls were knotted in a bandanna, black corkscrews spraying out the top of her head. Since it was her day off from her job as manager, clerk and stockwoman at the bookstore, she hadn't bothered with makeup and her small frame swam in baggy red shorts and a ratty purple tank top featuring a smart-ass bunny cartoon.

"I just want to make sure I bring the most up-to-date selections," she defended. "What do you think? Which one screams *buy me* louder? Bridal white or sweetheart pink?"

Larissa held up two separate gift bags, one flocked with roses and edged in white feathers, the other covered in foil hearts and sporting a lacy handle.

"Do you think guys care about the color of a girl's panties? All they're concerned with is how hot the contents are."

"Not my future customers," Larissa dismissed. She gave a disdainful little sniff. Then she ruined it by grinning when Chloe rolled her eyes.

"You're going to have to work on that snooty attitude

if you want to make it uptown," Chloe chided. "Cartright Hotels are known for bringing in the hoitiest of the toity and the richest of the bitches."

Chloe was right. Cartright Hotels were known worldwide for their themed resorts. They had a golf hotel, with its world-class eighteen-hole green in Palm Springs. They had a spa hotel in St. Tropez and a hunting lodge-styled resort in the Adirondacks. And now they were opening a romantic getaway here in South Carolina.

A romance hotel, right here in Larissa's backyard. It was totally meant to be.

"Are you sure this is what you want?" Chloe asked, not for the first time. For a woman who specialized in leaping with her eyes closed, Chloe was sure picky about doing height checks on Larissa's jumps.

"Romantic getaway, Chloe," Larissa cried out, waving the baby blue silk panties in her hand to punctuate the exclamation. "This location is totally made for me. It's my dream. I've put in the time. Eight years working in Mr. Murphy's bookstore. Four years perfecting my brand as a romance specialist and two more building the Romance Rules network."

Sure, she could settle for a small store somewhere else, but why? If she wanted great things to happen in her life, she had to *make* them happen. Nobody else was going to make her dreams come true. Romance Rule number one, *It's Every Princess for Herself.* This was her shot at her very own store in a fancy upscale place like Cartright Plaza. It was perfect for her.

She just had to convince the committee in charge of choosing the boutique vendors that she was the perfect choice for them. And convince herself that she wasn't jumping too high, given her lack of experience as a business owner.

"Have you told Mr. Murphy yet?" Chloe asked, referring to the man Larissa had worked for since high school.

"Not yet. But it won't be a big deal. I mean, he's retiring, so it's not like I'm leaving him in the lurch."

"But he's been hinting around that he'd like you to buy him out, hasn't he?"

Larissa's gleeful bubble of hope burst a little. She shrugged, tossing the blue silk panties into the case of lingerie.

"Sure, he'd sell me the business. But if I buy it, it's still his store, under new ownership, you know? I'd be keeping Mr. Murphy's dream alive, not living my own." Despite that, a part of her wanted to settle. She had enough money to make the down payment. When she'd first toyed with the idea of buying his store someday, she'd still been living with the wealthy aunt who'd raised her after Larissa's parents had died.

But then her aunt had died, leaving her home and all of her wealth to the Preservation of Feral Felines. And leaving Larissa homeless. Larissa had started saving money for her future, but working as a bookseller wasn't known as a road to riches.

She was sure Mr. Murphy would carry the rest of the loan for her. But she knew if she settled, she'd never take the leap. She'd always be reminded of her naive belief in happy-ever-after and thinking that some prince would sweep in and make her world perfect.

Nope. If she wanted her dreams, she had to make them happen herself. Now. She laid a hand on her queasy stomach.

"It's all for the best," she said, not sure if she was trying to convince herself or Chloe. "This way, I'm starting fresh. That's what I want. I mean, I think it's what I want…"

"You want it or you don't," Chloe pushed. "Decide. Then,

for crying out loud, quit second guessing yourself. You know what your problem is?"

"My choice in friends?"

"Don't be silly. You'd be miserable without me. You'd hole up with a stack of books and your dreams with the curtains closed while life flew by."

Larissa grinned, tilting her head in agreement. She couldn't argue with the truth. She loved nothing better than curling up with a romance novel, losing herself in the delights of happy-ever-after.

"Your problem is you think everything has to be perfect," Chloe said, tucking her feet under her as she lounged on the chair.

"What's wrong with perfect?"

"Nothing, as long as you realize that life isn't that tidy. If you're always holding out for some shiny image of perfection, you miss a lot of great living." Chloe gave her an arched look and shoved her hand through her long blond hair, purple nails glittering. The nails perfectly matched the zebra stripes in the magenta leggings she'd paired with her black tunic.

A freelance makeup artist, Chloe was the epitome of a free spirit. She went through life turning lemons into gourmet lemonade. The few times Larissa had tried to make the metaphorical drink, it'd damn near choked her. Given how badly she sucked at turning bad into good, she tried hard— really, really hard—to make sure her life was lemon-free.

"I live," Larissa defended.

"Sure you do. But it's like you've created this litmus test for life. There are some great things out there that aren't perfect, you know."

"Of course I know that. I live with you, don't I?"

Chloe snorted. "Good point. And okay, yes, Cartright

Plaza is a great fit for your dream store. It's almost as if Conner built it with you in mind."

"But he didn't," Larissa said quickly, trying to hide her grimace.

Conner Cartright and his brother, Daniel, ran the Cartright empire. When Larissa's parents had died in a car accident, she'd gone to live with her aunt, a wealthy, eccentric spinster. Conner was the poor little rich boy who'd lived up the street. He'd had a crush on her for a while, but he'd given it up after he realized she'd only ever see him as a buddy.

Their friendship had almost bit the dust two years ago, when a selfish *jerk,* incapable of understanding a mature relationship, had misconstrued their friendship, then used it to break Larissa's heart.

She ground her teeth together in frustration, as irritated at the memory as she was at the fact that it could still get her so worked up and angry. Seeing her expression, thankfully Chloe let the subject drop.

Instead, her friend dug into a box labeled Chloe's Fun that she'd hauled out of her closet when she'd seen Larissa's collection of boxes. She tossed a few items willy-nilly into Larissa's collection of merchandise already deemed worthy of displaying.

"What are you doing?" Larissa asked, grabbing one of the objects midflight.

"Sending you with a few of the Chloe Kits I made."

Larissa looked at the beautifully wrapped box in her hand. The silver paper glinted and the velvet bow added just the right touch of elegance above the label stating the box contained One Romantic Evening.

Knowing Chloe, that meant a tiny bottle of tequila, a handful of flavored condoms and an edible guy-size thong.

Larissa didn't bother to sigh. Instead she set the box on

the table and decided to go with the pink bag and lace undies she'd been considering earlier.

"What's the deal?" Chloe asked, her voice rising. "I thought you loved my kits? Are you really afraid your future customers won't be looking for a good time?"

"I'm selling the promise of a happy-ever-after, Chloe. I'm not going to dilute it with gratuitous sex."

"Sex doesn't dilute, it spices things up." With that, Chloe tossed a few of her kits into the keeper box. Larissa gave up, figuring it wasn't worth the argument she'd hear if she took them out. "And even you, the ambassador of pure romance, have to admit that lovin' is better spicy."

"I don't need sex to make my point," Larissa insisted half-heartedly. Through with the gift selection, she turned to one of the multitude of bookcases lining the living room wall to choose which of the hundreds of romance novels and self-help books she wanted to feature.

"You mean you don't want to use sex to prove your point," Chloe said, getting up to go into the kitchen and grab some chips to snack on. "But it is an important part of romance. You keep trying to gloss over it and you'll end up with some sterile, boring ode to platonic fantasies. I mean, yuck."

Larissa lowered two handfuls of books to stare, open-mouthed, as her roommate returned with a bag of crisp, cheesy potato goodness.

"Yuck?"

Who the hell yucked romance?

"Yes, yuck. Would you really want a sexless romance?" Her emerald-and-turquoise MAC shadowed lids glittering, Chloe's eye roll was a work of art.

"I'm not saying I want sexless romance. I'm just saying I don't think sex is the number-one priority."

"I'll bet your customers think sex is a priority," Chloe said, crunching away, then licking chip dust off her fingers.

It was like talking to a stubborn three-year-old. Larissa slapped her fists on her narrow hips and glared at her oldest friend.

"Quit, already," she insisted, starting to feel bruised from the constant poking. "It's not that I think sex doesn't count. But that's not what I'm selling. Isn't It Romantic is all about teaching men, and yes, women, to pay attention to the sweet little gestures and tender moments that make a relationship special."

"And I'm not saying that *those* things don't count," Chloe said in the long-suffering tone of patience she'd perfected in her teens. "I'm just saying that if you keep shuffling sex to the bottom of your priority list—or worse, trying to hide it in the closet—you're going to lose out. Both personally and professionally."

"Look, my store is going to be called Isn't It Romantic. Not Prudes R Us. Quit making it sound like I have something against sex."

"But...don't you?"

Larissa blinked a couple times. Then she bent over a box of cozy blankets, unfolding and testing out the different mohair and cashmere blends to see which one she wanted to bring. She finally decided on a lush, white angora blend that felt like a cloud of silk in her fingers, adding it to her display box.

"You make it sound like I'm some kind of nun. I'm not. Aren't all of my favorite romance novels hot and spicy? There's nothing more satisfying than reading about hot tension, the building intensity, then an explosive, um..." Even though the two women were alone in the apartment, she still lowered her voice to a whisper, "climax."

"See! You can't even say it."

"Oh, bull," she shot back in her normal tone. "I love sex."

At least, she loved the memory of sex. It'd been a while since she'd loved it firsthand. Not for lack of interest or out of any sexual prejudice. But a girl got busy, focusing on her career, and there just wasn't much time left over for the frills.

"When was the last time you got any?" Chloe challenged.

Larissa opened her mouth to shoot back a snappy retort, then clamped her lips together. Answering would only prove Chloe's point. Instead, she said, "When was the last time you had any that was good enough to be in a romance novel?"

Larissa didn't need an answer. She knew she'd won. Heck, she regularly listened to Chloe's complaints about lousy sex. Heck, she'd used it in at least a half dozen of her romance columns.

Of course, that's not all she talked about. After all, she'd had plenty of personal experience with mind-blowing, life-altering, headboard-banging sex. Her very own romance novel sex. But that'd been a lot of years ago and she'd learned the hard way that there had to be more. Trust, companionship, common goals. Those things might not make her scream in ecstasy, but they sure went a lot further to making the romance long term than a triple chocolate-dipped orgasm.

"Look, I'm just saying you have to consider a wider clientele than just you," Chloe said, giving Larissa's shoulder a quick squeeze. "Just because you've chosen to bury your sexual needs beneath eight layers of romantic fluff doesn't mean everyone will. Isn't the purpose of this business to succeed?"

"Of course I plan to succeed," Larissa said, ignoring both Chloe's point and the panic clutching at her own belly. "I know what I'm doing."

"I do, too. You're ignoring an automatic tie-in with your store's theme because you've got issues with sex."

Finished avoiding the topic, Larissa dropped onto the rocking chair, folded her arms over her chest and got her pout on.

"I don't have issues."

"How would you know? It's been so long since you had any, you can't even test that theory out."

Larissa's pout deepened. She dug her chin into her chest and stared at the perfection of her French pedicure. "Maybe I don't have a sex drive."

Chloe's snort bounced off the walls. "Right."

"Maybe we all peak at different times," she defended before her friend could explain the reasons behind her snort. Some things were better left unsaid. "Maybe I hit my peak and now I just have to accept that my sex drive is on the way down."

Chloe sighed, then uncurled her long body from the round chair and crossed the room to give Larissa a hug. She kneeled and offered a long, serious look at odds with her wild appearance.

"Or maybe you're giving Jason Cantrell too much credit. It's not like he has a magic dick, Larissa. It wasn't coated with orgasm glitter or anything."

Larissa wrinkled her nose. Not at the crude expression. She was so used to Chloe's vernacular, she barely noticed. Nope, her wince was over the mention of Jason's name.

"If you were a nurse, you'd be the kind who grinned over giving people shots in the ass, wouldn't you?" Larissa said with a narrowed look.

"Why?" Chloe challenged, her lips twitching at the accusation. "Because hearing Jason's name hurts you somehow?"

"I'm not hurting."

Chloe waited.

Larissa closed her eyes for a moment.

Sure, she might not trust men anymore. She might lie awake at night, wondering if she'd ever have the perfect storybook romance like those she read about. And maybe she was a little wary of being called out as a fraud for not having any real romance in her personal life. But that wasn't hurt.

It was more like a cute pink bandage over the top of a big ugly scab hiding a three-year-old boo-boo.

She winced. Okay, so maybe she wasn't completely over him. But she mostly was, and that's what counted.

"Maybe I'm a little cautious," she finally acknowledged. "But that only applies to my personal life. Not to my business."

"But you're letting your hurt and bad feelings over your breakup with Jason color your business choices, aren't you?"

Larissa pressed her lips together, wanting to deny it. But she was a lousy liar.

"Sometimes I feel like a fraud," Larissa confessed. "Who am I to claim to be an authority on romance when my one and only relationship failed."

"If you could do it over again, would you have done anything different?" Chloe asked. "Kicked him where it would hurt, maybe? Or defended yourself when he accused you of cheating?"

"Why should I have to defend myself?" she replied. "He should have trusted me. Without trust, there is no relationship."

"Hey, I'm not defending the guy," Chloe denied. "He broke your heart, he deserves to die. I'm just saying that maybe it's time to let it go."

Larissa stared down at her tangled fingers, remembering

the short—less than a week, short—time a diamond had sparkled there. A part of her had known when Jason had given her the ring that their engagement wouldn't last. There were just too many differences between them. But she'd hoped. Oh, how she'd hoped.

Chloe, obviously realizing she'd made her point—and was in danger of delving into tequila-healing territory when Larissa couldn't afford to do the presentation with a hangover—changed the subject.

"All I'm saying is that if there is a way to guarantee your store has a better chance of surviving the first year, you should do it. And widening your focus just a bit would increase those odds," Chloe persuaded.

"No." She crossed her arms over her chest and lifted her chin. She'd had this dream for too long. "I'm not going to ruin my dream with a compromise I'll hate."

"Bending, just a little, doesn't mean you're caving," Chloe said quietly. "Remember, Mr. Murphy offered to let you buy his store when he retires next month. If you're not willing to change your concept, maybe you should consider a lower rent venue. Because once you make this choice, there's no going back."

The safety of that was so appealing. Larissa loved the old Victorian that housed Mr. Murphy's bookstore. She'd nursed her love of romances there, built her skills as a communicator and a salesperson. She was safe there…as long as she did things his way, kept with the same old program. But if she changed things? Would people come? Would she lose the bulk of the tried and true customers who had expectations that she couldn't meet anymore because she was pursuing her own hopes and dreams?

Larissa looked at the mess she'd made of boxes, books and all of the accoutrements she deemed necessary for romance. Even though this time she was risking her career and her finances, it was still as difficult as it had been with her heart. But this time, she knew what she was doing. She wasn't falling in love without a clue, she was prepared.

"I can do this," she said decisively. And she'd consider the sex stuff, too. Maybe this was her chance. Time to change her business, and her personal life. She was through hiding behind the past, waiting for Prince Charming. She was putting "get a sex life" on her agenda, dammit. Right after she dealt with her career, of course.

Determined, she stood and put the lid on her box of merchandise. She was as ready as she was going to get. "But I need to decide what to wear. Want to help me pick out the perfect snooty outfit?"

Chloe rose, studying her carefully. Then she gave a slow nod. "Sure. I specialize in snoot."

See, Larissa thought as they headed for her bedroom and its overcrowded closet. She'd prove, to Chloe and to herself, that she didn't need a magic dick to make her dreams come true.

# 2

JASON CANTRELL HANDLED HIS BMW like he was on a racetrack. Fast, tight and controlled. He hit the freeway off-ramp doing eighty, Aerosmith's rhythm beating through the speakers like a war drum.

He spared a glance at the clock on the dash.

Late.

He gave a mental shrug. No point wasting energy on what he couldn't change.

His plane had been delayed, then he'd got caught up in customs where he'd had to explain the three-foot penis he'd brought back from the Papua New Guinea. Well, maybe not so much explain, since the kotekas, or penis-sheaths, were pretty self-explanatory. Still, his was special.

Aerosmith's walking instructions were interrupted when the Bluetooth in Jason's dash pounded out its own beat. He flicked a button on the steering wheel.

"Yo," he answered.

"Yo, yourself. How'd the meeting go?"

A quick glance noted there was no traffic. With a flick of his wrist Jason took a corner at twice the speed limit.

"I'm on my way, big brother," he said. "I called Daniel when I landed and told him I'd be late. He's missing this meet but said he'd pass the message on to the committee. Don't worry, the pitch practically sells itself. We've got it in the bag."

"I'm not worried about the pitch," Peter said. "You could sell snow to a polar bear. I'm just... Well... You know."

Ever the wordsmith, that was Peter Cantrell. Jason gave a rueful shake of his head.

"I know. It's going to work out. Quit stressing, okay."

It, being their business. A business the two brothers had started at twenty-two and twenty, respectively. They'd grown up traveling with their archaeologist parents and were on their second passport before they'd hit puberty. At first, the brothers had led a few buddies on trips as a way to make beer money in college. Mountain climbing, rafting, hiking. Soon they'd developed a rep for creating awesome adventures. They had inside knowledge of places they'd already visited and they made it a point to turn each trip into a special event. That beer money had quickly turned to seed money. They were doing so well that by the time Peter graduated, Jason had dropped out to take on Can-Do Adventures full-time.

But now they needed to make some changes. Because he wanted to settle down with his fiancée and play happy hubby, Peter had decided to take a step back from the regular trips. Only neither brother wanted to hire help. They couldn't control the quality of a trip halfway around the world unless one of them was leading it. Which meant cutting their income in half...unless they found a way to advertise to a higher-paying group of adventurers and woo in some bigger groups.

Hence, Cartright Hotels. If they snagged this store, they could easily tap into the promotional benefits of the hotel conglomerate, entice the wealthy clientele and support both brothers on the same number of trips led just by Jason. Cartright was offering a primo deal, advertising their newest businesses in their press packets for the first year. They were doing ads in airline and travel magazines, linking their loyalty points to the use of their own vendors—of which Can-Do would be one, if Jason played his cards right—and launching a huge media blitz.

In return, the Cantrells would add specialized/couple adventures, exclusive to Cartright guests, to their repertoire. Adventure honeymoons and wild getaways. All at vastly discounted rates, if booked while staying at one of Cartright's resorts.

An all-round win-win deal, if he did say so himself.

"You sure you want to do this?" Peter asked. "I mean, if they don't go for it, we can still salvage the business. I'll kick in part of my income to keep things afloat, and continue to handle the bookings after you find another partner."

Peter had just lined up a job with a local sports store, selling equipment, teaching rock climbing, basically catering to the weekend warriors. Jason knew his brother hated the idea, but he needed the income. It was yet another reason to make this deal with Cartwright work—Peter could man the store instead of selling tennis shoes and ski equipment. It really sucked that his brother had been talked into becoming more "steady."

"I don't want another partner," Jason dismissed. He didn't dismiss the offer to supplement Can-Do's income, though. He knew damned well that between the business and family expenses, he couldn't carry it all on his own.

A few years back, their mother had a stroke that had not only physically debilitated her, but had also destroyed her marriage. Because neither brother was able to take care of her themselves, Jason and Peter had been forced to choose between the depressing rehab center her insurance would cover, or ponying up to put her in a nice, cheerful housing program.

Ever their father's son, Peter's first suggestion when he'd said he needed to step down at Can-Do was to move their mother to the less-expensive assisted living unit. That'd been one of the few times Jason had blown up at his brother.

So now it was up to him to make sure everything worked out.

"We'll make it happen," he vowed. "I know I can pull this off."

"Well, you'd never find a partner as good as me, so I don't blame you," Peter joked. His tone was still stressed, though. Like he wasn't sure if he should push his brother to go it alone or take him at his word.

"You're hard to beat," Jason agreed. "Of course, I'm still the best."

"You wish." Peter laughed, sounding relieved. "Are you sure you don't want me to meet you, help with the pitch?"

"Nah, I've got it. Between the pitch and showing them the koteka as an example of the kinds of things we'd display, I'm sure it's in the bag. Besides…you've got enough to do. I'll come by in the morning and let you know how it goes," he promised. "You get the coffee ready and I'll bring my penis."

"Mine's still bigger," Peter promised.

Jason's smile slipped as the phone turned off and Aerosmith's "Sweet Emotion" filled his ears. The endless competition was just one more thing he was going to miss if Peter didn't come to his senses before the dreaded I Do-Day.

And the chances of that were looking sadly slim. Not that Jason had anything against Meghan, the sweet little thing his brother was marrying. But they already lived together. Peter was getting all the goodies—why sign on for the long haul? Especially when that haul meant ruining Can-Do Adventures.

Jason was going to have to run the business alone if

this little brainstorm didn't play out the way he wanted. Because he'd be damned if he'd take on a new partner. He liked doing things his way, on his own terms. Besides, he knew damned well that relationships didn't last. So it was his job as a good brother to keep things going so Peter had something to do when the Meghan deal went belly-up.

Ready to pitch and win, Jason pulled into the almost-empty parking lot, tires squealing. He parked next to a little red Mini S convertible, bounded from his car and strode toward the building.

A quick glance told him the location was prime. The almost completed hotel to the right, the city's business district three blocks past the park on the left. The place would pull in travelers and upscale shoppers alike. And all of them were potential customers for a Can-Do Adventure. More importantly, Peter could manage the store until he came to his senses and got back to living life to the fullest.

And in the meantime? They needed to make enough money to keep Can-Do afloat and cover their mother's expenses. Which meant not only cutting their tours in half without Peter, but slashing their promotion budget.

And that was where Cartright Hotels came in. It wasn't the location alone that had Jason excited. It was the promotion package offered to the vendors. Co-op, inclusion in Cartright's worldwide advertising, massively discounted television ads. One year here would set Can-Do up for the decade. It was plenty of time for Peter to get his head together.

All Jason had to do was snag that last store space.

No problem. Daniel Cartwright was a good friend. He and Peter had been frat buddies. The Cantrells had lived up the street—on the poorer side—from the Cartrights growing up, too. They hadn't actually run in the same circles, but Dan was a good guy even if his younger brother, Conner, was a jerk. No matter who else he had on the hook for the storefront, Jason was sure Can-Do was the frontrunner.

And just in case? He gripped the padded crate under his arm and grinned. Daniel said the hotel, and its adjoining boutique mall, were an ode to coupledom. Not something Jason had much experience with since his one attempt had been a huge bust. But he figured the one thing couples all wanted was a good sex life, so he'd brought his secret weapon. The koteka was supposed to be magic. The promise was that it'd bring blessings and hot sex to the wearer. Jason figured that if the Powers That Be weren't bowled over with his pitch, he could offer the koteka as an incentive. After all, what guy could resist the promise of hot sex?

That, his charm and the brilliance of his idea were all he'd need to snag this space and settle his life back on the track he wanted. Can-Do Adventures would survive. Neither storms nor mechanical failures nor a commitment-seeking woman would stop the brothers from their appointed purpose. Which was to see as much, do as much and discover as much of the world as possible.

In other words, to live. Free and easy. The only way to be.

"THIS IS STUNNING," Larissa said breathlessly, laying her hand on Conner's arm. She stared, wide-eyed, taking in the glorious view. Lush plants decorated the long, posh concourse of the mall. The floors were glossy marble. The walls were papered in rich silk. The windows glinted like diamonds and the entire space shouted exclusivity.

And her store would be here. It was like fantasizing about being swept away by a pirate, then finding herself on a deserted island with Johnny Depp. A dream come true, multiplied by a hundred.

"La Perla, Armani, Godiva," she murmured, shivering

in delight as she read the gilt signs already above some of the stores. She squinted, imagining Isn't It Romantic tucked up there between such stellar names, and grinned.

The place was small by mall standards, only eighty thousand square feet, but it didn't feel that way. The wide concourse with its lush greenery and center benches gave the feel of an outdoor garden. Only five stores on either side lined the concourse, with two discreet hallways angling off to the restrooms and the employee maintenance area.

She turned to face the man who used to be one of her best friends, but whom she hadn't seen much of in the last two years. Not since the *big ugly fiasco,* as she mentally referred to the worst night of her life.

She was glad Conner seemed to be over the whole humiliating incident and was willing to not only see her again, but to give her such an incredible opportunity. Still, she didn't figure reminding him of the *big ugly fiasco* was a good idea.

So instead, she gave him a cautious smile. "Conner, this is all so fabulous. You and Daniel must be so proud of the hotel, and of this mall."

"I'm actually quite proud of what I'm about to pull off," he said. His smile was innocuous enough, but there was something in his tone that caught Larissa's attention. She narrowed her eyes, wondering what he was up to. But then he added, "Want to see the space that's available?"

"My store?" she queried, only half teasing. "Heck, yeah."

"Right this way."

Her wheeled cart carrying the boxes of sample merchandise squeaked behind her as she let Conner lead her to the only store with its arched, glass doors open wide. Her breath hitched. She blinked quickly to clear the sudden tears from her eyes.

It was perfect.

Large, bright and, oh man, so, so luxurious. The counters were granite. The walls were lined with gilt-framed mirrors. She could see a dressing room off to the back and a sign indicating a bathroom. Other than the checkout counters, the room was empty except for a deeply cushioned settee against one wall. She spun around to check the view as she imagined herself behind the counter thanking her customers.

Just perfect. Through the pristine front windows, she could see the lush plants surrounding a plush velvet bench and a statue of Aphrodite, just inside the hotel lobby.

Larissa's Romance Rule number one: Appearances count. And appearing here would count for so much. Thrilled, she hugged herself tight.

"So, is it what you were hoping for?" Conner asked. "Can you imagine writing your column from the Cartright Boutique? Romance à la Cartright, catchy, huh?"

Larissa's brow went up before she could stop it. He was kidding, right? But she managed to keep the question to herself. Old friend or not, pissing Conner off was a bad idea. Cartright's policy was to promote all the stores on their properties on their website, in their other venues and with little gifts and special mailings to their patrons. There was no way she could ever afford that level of marketing on her own. The only way to get it was to snag this store space.

"Is that my new byline? The Romance Authority, brought to you by Cartright Hotels?" Her joking tone faded as she saw that he was serious. She knew that promotion was a big deal for Cartright, and that by taking a space in the mall, she'd be included in the co-op.

But this? She wasn't sure how she felt about it. It felt wrong, somehow. Like she was selling out.

Conner must have sensed her hesitation, because he

laughed it off and gave her shoulder a quick pat before stepping away. "I'll give you time to set up your display, hmm? The committee is meeting in a half hour. Would you mind coming back to the boardroom then to give your presentation?"

A little confused and conflicted, Larissa silently nodded, then watched him leave. It wasn't until she heard the echo of the elevator door closing in the empty mall that she let out her breath and looked around again.

Then realizing that she only had thirty minutes to make the store scream Isn't It Romantic, she shoved her worry to the back of her mind and got to work. After all, seeing was believing. She was sure the committee would fall in love with her store as soon as they saw how well her lovely merchandise fit in their exclusive space.

FORTY MINUTES LATER, Conner nervously fiddled with his pen as he listened to Larissa's pitch. He shifted in his chair, then adjusted his tie. The third time he ran his hand over his hair, he elbowed his marketing VP, Ben Jackson, giving him the evil eye.

Time to chill. Conner forced himself to calm down and act like the responsible, clear-headed businessman he usually was. He had too much on the line—both with this hotel and mall, and with his own private scheme—to blow it now.

They were in one of his newly completed hotel boardrooms, just Larissa and the three-man committee who would decide the fate of her dream. Conner had hand chosen the two men on the committee. Both were golfing buddies and good friends. But more important, both had a decent level of acting skills, which were vital if his scheme was going to work.

"Gentlemen," Larissa said with a charming smile that

made Conner want to sigh. "Your focus on couples, honeymoon packages and romantic getaways ties in perfectly with my store. Isn't It Romantic will totally enhance your guests' stay. I'll stock romance books, both fiction and nonfiction. Romantic movies through the ages. All the necessary accoutrements to bringing the pleasure of romance into your—our—guests' visit, as well as providing them with mementos of their wonderful stay that they'll appreciate for years to come."

As she continued, Conner let himself get distracted by how she looked. The same as the last time he'd seen her, yet, not quite. Her hair, often a riot of wild curls, was a tame fall of ringlets framing her sharp face. She wore a black suit, its austere color softened by a ruffled jacket and a skirt that hugged her hips and legs to the knee, where it echoed the jacket's ruffle. The darkness of her clothing was offset by vivid red heels that sent a few fantasies skittering through Conner's head before he reminded himself that he didn't think of Larissa that way.

Drew Franklin, the guy on his left, kicked him under the table. Conner started, then remembered the game. His plan was to keep her off balance until the, well, the surprise he'd been calling it. She might refer to it as the big betrayal. Or the knife in her back. Maybe some other title that included ugly swear words.

No matter, he owed her. And a Cartright always paid his dues.

"Larissa, this sounds great. The committee has a few questions, though," Conner said. He kept his voice a little distant instead of encouraging.

He hated to see her smile dim, nerves clear in her eyes as she nodded and said, "Of course. I'd be happy to answer them."

"It's a nice idea, I agree. But why just romance?" Drew

Franklin asked, embracing his role as the doubtful hard-ass. "Why such a narrow focus?"

"My impression was that you were looking for boutiques, not department stores," Larissa said, sounding a little less like a polished businesswoman and a little more like the spunky girl Conner knew. Good, she was going to need that spunk today.

"Sure. Boutiques are the goal. But couldn't you diversify a bit? You know, maybe spice it up or something?" he prodded.

"Or something?"

"You know, something sexier." He said it like sexier was a euphemism for kink on a stick.

Larissa wrinkled her nose, looking like she wanted to ask if he was a member of the pervert-of-the-month club. Conner looked down at his blank notepad to hide his grin.

"I do understand the appeal of diversification," she said after a deep breath. "And if you consider it, you'll see that I have diversified in a big way. Isn't It Romantic is more than a bookstore, or a movie store, or one focusing only on candles and scents. It's got it all."

Apparently deciding it was time to wow them with her charts and diagrams, Larissa handed each man a folder containing sketches, swatches and photos of the array of items she planned to carry.

"This is great," Ben said, flipping through the contents enthusiastically. He gave Larissa a flirtatious look, making her smile dim. She shot Conner a baffled, do-you-only-employ-creeps look.

He resisted the urge to pump his fist in the air. His plan was working. The worse he made guys look in the next half hour, the better she'd respond to his surprise.

He hoped. If not, his brother Daniel was going to seriously kick his ass for scaring away not one, but two perfect candidates for the storefront.

"Ben's right," Conner agreed. "You've really nailed the concept here. I think your idea is unique and would fit in nicely with Cartright's message."

"I still think it's a little, well, boring," Drew said, starting to tap his pen on the unopened folder she'd given him. "If a couple is staying at this locale, they're already covered with that romance thing. They want spice. They want excitement. They want—"

"I don't think romance ends when a couple checks into the hotel unless he's paying her by the hour," Larissa said with an arched brow. Then she smiled. "But that isn't really romance, is it? Or the type of hotel you're opening?"

Conner tried to disguise his laugh as a cough. Ben wasn't quite as successful.

"But I can see where you're coming from," she said, obviously encouraged that two-thirds of the room seemed to be on her side. "And I guarantee that Isn't It Romantic would cover the gamut of tastes, from sweet to spicy."

"Ms. Zahn, I think I speak for all of us when I say you've made a strong impression. Your store would align nicely with the other business we've chosen to represent us at the Cartright," Ben told her.

Conner nodded while Drew had pasted on an over-the-top bored look.

"I'd love for you to see what I have in mind for the space," she offered quickly. She placed her hand on the large box she'd carried in. "I've brought a few of the items I'd stock with me and I've created a display in the store that will give you a better understanding of the atmosphere and aesthetic I'll bring to the South Carolina Cartright."

Ben nodded enthusiastically. Drew gave a sigh, though,

as if getting up and walking to the elevators was more work than he'd intended to do today.

Before Conner could add his own two cents, a message flashed on his cell phone. He read it and grinned. Perfect. He looked at his colleagues and gestured with the phone.

"I just received the message that our earlier appointment has finally arrived. This is great. We can wrap up the interviews now, before heading out for the weekend," Conner said. "Larissa, if you'd please wait in the antechamber, we'll head down to the mall to look at your display just as soon as we finish with this appointment."

He offered Larissa an innocent smile and said, "Our next interview won't be long. Would you mind making yourself comfortable?"

She frowned, then with a quick shrug, gathered her charts and diagrams and tucked them away in her briefcase. She gave him a couple of searching looks, like she was trying to see what he was up to—or was that just his guilty conscience?

He wanted to rush the table and wrap her in his arms, assuring her that he'd make everything right for her.

Larissa had always had that effect on him. She was so pretty, with her riotous black curls and huge, dark eyes. He'd had a crush on her ever since he was fourteen, when she'd moved in with her eccentric aunt up the street.

Unfortunately, he'd made the mistake of acting on that attraction, only to be rebuffed in the most painful way—with sweet pity. And he'd reacted poorly. Acting like a spoiled brat, he'd lashed out. Not at her, but at the fiancé she'd refused to leave for him, hinting to the other man that there was something more going on between him and Larissa. Conner had felt justified, since they broke up. For about a week. Then he'd felt like shit. His greedy obnoxiousness had hurt two people, one of whom he cared about deeply.

He was hoping to make it up to her now. By tomorrow, she'd either love him again—as a friend. Or hate him.

FOLLOWING THE DIRECTIONS Daniel Cartright had given him, Jason made his way through the empty hotel. He glanced at his cell phone to check his battery. It was heading for dead, but probably had enough juice for him to offer up a convincing slideshow during the presentation.

Looking forward to seeing Daniel, who, after rooming with Jason's brother for three years in college, was as much Jason's buddy as Peter's, Jason sauntered into the boardroom with a wide grin on his face. The grin faded as he stepped through the doorway.

Instead of finding Daniel sitting at the head of the shiny new boardroom table, Jason was greeted by his younger brother, Conner.

Jason barely noticed the other two guys flanking him. He was too focused on the sudden fury flashing through his brain.

Memories washed over him like a monsoon. Larissa. Damn, he'd fallen hard and intense for her. He'd been young enough, stupid enough, to think he'd been in love with her. Their affair had been hot, wild and intense. Until she'd cheated on him with Conner.

Bombarded by feelings he'd been sure were long gone, he clenched his teeth and resisted the urge to tear into the guy.

His shoulders clenched, his hands fisting at his sides. He was being ridiculous, he reminded himself. Conner had been in Europe, not aware that Jason and Larissa were a thing when he'd asked her out. And when he'd found out, he'd completely backed off. Conner wasn't to blame. Larissa was.

On the surface, Jason and Conner had made their peace

a couple years ago. The past was over. And if there was one thing Jason prided himself on, it was being the kind of guy who didn't dwell on stuff that was already put away. Especially not anything as useless as emotional baggage.

Especially not now, when he had a business to save.

"Hey, Conner," Jason greeted, his words only a little stiff. He forced himself to stride through the wide-open doors of the partially furnished boardroom. "This is a surprise. I thought I was meeting with Daniel."

Conner, looking like the successful tycoon he'd always been, rose with a smile to shake Jason's hand. For a brief, stomach-churning second, Jason could see why Larissa would go for the guy. He was just like one of those romance novel heroes.

Stop, Jason mentally snapped at himself. Focusing on the past was useless. Put it away and make today happen.

"Jason, good to see you. Unfortunately, Daniel was called away and couldn't be here. But we're glad you could make it. Since we're running behind, let me introduce you to the committee and we'll get started. Then we can catch up later, if you'd like."

"Sure thing." But before Conner could say anything else Jason made his way around the table, and with handshakes all around, introduced himself.

He dropped the case holding his trump card, so to speak, onto the polished table, barely noting the tufts of dust that rose as it hit the wood.

"Have a seat," one of the committee members suggested. "Conner's told us about your ideas and I'll admit, I'm loving the prospect of working with you. But we have another contender for the space and we are in a bit of a hurry. So if you don't mind, grab a seat and tell us about your plans."

Jason eyed Conner, wondering just what he'd told the committee. Daniel had taken a few trips with Can-Do. But

Conner wasn't really the roughing-it type, so he'd always passed. Sure, they were all cool now. But given that, at one time, Jason had threatened to toss Conner out a window, he wouldn't have been surprised if the dude still held a grudge.

Nice to know they were both too big for that kind of crap, Jason thought, giving Conner a friendly smile. Then, parking the past into the history books where it belonged, he focused on the here, now and more importantly, the future.

"I'll skip the sitting invite, if you don't mind," he told the partner. "I just flew in from the Galapagos by way of Zimbabwe, so my ass is pretty numb."

"Pace away, my friend," Conner said with a wave of his hand. "I'd love to hear about your latest trip, too. But Ben has a plane to catch, so why don't you give us your pitch before he goes."

Jason gave a friendly nod. "No problem. First off, I'd like to say thank you to all of you for considering Can-Do Adventures. Regardless of whether we end up working as a team here at the latest Cartright Hotel, I hope you'll all accept an invitation to take a trip as our gift. Any adventure, from the Andes to Tanzania, just give us a call and we'll set it up."

Jason reminded himself to let his brother know. Peter was the money-man, which meant he'd probably throw a fit at the thousands Jason had just tossed on the table. But it was worth the gamble. Besides, if they didn't get this space, Can-Do would be Used-To, so it wouldn't matter.

"What makes you think a travel agency would thrive in a hotel catering to couples?" the pudgy, less-friendly guy asked.

"Fair question. Ben, isn't it?" Jason stuffed his hands in his front pockets and rocked back on the worn heels of his hiking boots, waiting for the guy to nod.

"First off, Can-Do isn't a typi[...] [tr]avel agency. We don't book cruises and family trips. [...] [speci]alize in adventure. In thrills and excitement and push[...] [li]mits [...] [t]wo bookings are alike, since no two peop[...] [...]g. We customize one-of-a-kind tours. A[...] [...]ied with the Cartright Hotels, we'll be offering ve[ry] [ex]clusive, very impressive tours for Cartright's patrons."

He emphasized that point, since it was one that was near and dear to his heart. It was also the first one that'd have to go if this deal didn't come through. He pictured himself leading his tenth hike of the month through the Daintree Rainforest, on a first-name basis with the tree-kangaroos, and shuddered. Gorgeous, yes. But with that kind of repetition, there was no excitement. Travel for the sake of seeing the same thing over and over was as bad as sitting on his ass in front of a television watching the nature channel.

Totally not his thing.

Not that he hadn't considered it, once. Giving up the wild trips, playing it safe. Or at least, safer. He'd almost left Peter in the same lurch his brother now had him in. That was why he couldn't be too pissed at the guy. Women—some very special women—could make a man go stupid.

Jason eyed Conner and wondered if he should've thanked the guy all those years ago instead of getting ugly. After all, if Conner hadn't swooped in with his rich boy charm and swept Larissa away, who knew what kind of craziness Jason might have gotten into?

But he'd learned his lesson. And his brother probably would, too. That was the reason Jason had to seal this deal— so they both had a career when Peter came to his senses. Or got bored playing house, whichever came first.

"Can-Do is the perfect pairing for the Cartright Hotel. Your clientele is used to the best, and we're it. They're used to being catered to, and we excel in catering. And by aligning with us in this location, we'll offer the same discounts and packages to the patrons in all of your venues. In addition, we'll create a deeply discounted Cartright Exclusive weekend adventure package."

He went on to explain how Can-Do would utilize the space, more like a small museum, which would be more appealing than the bland travel agency storefront many would expect. Showcasing artifacts, curios and specialty items from the many places they offered tours, the space would act as a Can-Do maintained attraction for the hotel guests.

Jason finished his pitch with the videos on his phone, then told them about the antique penis sheath he'd brought back from Papua New Guinea as an example of the quality of merchandise they'd show in the store.

"Jason, this is fabulous. You've given us a lot to think about." Conner glanced at the two men, one of whom was making a show of looking at his watch. "If you don't mind, we need to talk for a minute before Ben has to go. Would you be so good as to wait in the antechamber while we tie up some loose ends? Then we'll let you see the space for yourself."

"Sure thing," Jason said. He thanked the other two men, exchanged a few quips, then noticing Ben looked like he was about to explode, he graciously gathered his koteka under one arm and sauntered into the antechamber.

Still riding high with the success of his presentation, he caught a glimpse of movement across the room. The scent hit him before he turned. Soft roses, with an underlying layer of sexy heat. It made him think of making wild love in a garden under the full moon.

Crazy, he told himself as he stepped fully into the room and let the door swing shut behind him.

Then his brain sputtered. His heart raced as if he'd just

taken a long, deadly dive off a high cliff. His muscles tightened, his senses on full-alert. It took Jason's body a few extra seconds to filter the rush of energy flying through his system. Lust mixed with shock. Memories cascaded like a waterfall, pouring over forgotten hopes and hurts.

Sonofabitch.

Thickly lashed brown eyes, tilted like a startled cat's at the corners, stared back at him. He recognized the horror in her gaze, just as he recognized the flash of hot desire beneath it. Pale color rose, washing over her high cheekbones.

It'd been two years. And still, he could perfectly remember how those silky curls felt in his fingers. He knew exactly how that wide, mobile mouth would feel on his skin. He could see that lush little body stripped of its frilly black suit, naked and poised over the hard length of his.

He rocked back on his heels and grinned.

"Well, well," he murmured. "If it isn't the luscious Larissa. Who knew hell would freeze over this quickly?"

## 3

"JASON?"

Larissa stood, pressing her hand against the freshly painted wall trying to steady herself while the room spun wildly. She blinked. If she hadn't been afraid taking her hand from the wall would result in falling on her ass, she'd have rubbed her eyes.

She was hallucinating, right? This was a dream? A mirage brought on by her insistence that sex didn't matter. Payback for arguing against something she secretly lay awake at night fantasizing about?

Damn Chloe.

Slowly, reluctantly, Larissa slid her gaze over the illusion—or was that delusion—in the doorway. Six-foot-two of long, lean sexual magnetism. Unable to stop herself, she took in the sight. From the sun-kissed tips of his shaggy brown hair to the enigmatic look in his too-pretty-to-belong-to-a-guy blue eyes. Her fingers twitched with the need to comb them through those silken strands and push that one recalcitrant lock off his forehead.

She nearly sighed as she took in the view of his wide, muscled shoulders, wrapped in a soft cotton workshirt that perfectly matched those hypnotic eyes. His broad chest, with that light dusting of hair visible above the top button, was better than any pillow on earth. Her eyes dropped down to the well-worn denim lovingly covering his...

Oh, God. Larissa ripped her gaze from his crotch, where she was pretty sure she'd just visually licked him.

If she wasn't careful, she'd actually be climbing over his body and nibbling on all of his man parts before she knew it. He had that effect on her. He was danger, pure and simple.

It was all Larissa could do not to run from the room and yell for Conner.

Conner was safe.

Conner was her friend.

Conner was the reason she and Jason had so painfully split up two years ago.

No, she corrected herself. Jason himself was the reason behind their breakup. Him and his lack of trust.

She frowned, the wheels of her brain starting to turn again. Why was Jason here? Conner knew their history. Why would he—or any other sane person—bring the two of them together in the same room?

Conner was obviously an idiot, she decided.

"What are you doing here?" she asked after clearing the shock from her throat. "Shouldn't you be swinging from a vine in some jungle with a half-naked woman attached to your waist?"

He looked just as shocked as she was. And, from the heated glance in his eyes, he'd been sucked right into that same evil sexual vortex that had caused them both so many problems in the past.

"I left my loincloth with Jane," he responded in an absent tone. His attention was clearly more focused on his inspection of her body than on taking insult with her question. "You're looking good, though."

Larissa trembled, her thighs quivering a little at the sexy heat in Jason's eyes. God, that's all it took from him, a single look and she melted. He was like a fairy tale hero out of one of her favorite romance novels.

"So, obviously you and Conner are still tight," he said, crossing his arms over his chest.

Larissa's lusty reaction burst as if she'd been drenched in an ice bath. Her shoulders stiffened and she jutted out her chin. Romance hero, her ass.

"Obviously," she replied in a chilly tone.

If that's what he wanted to think, good. He was still a mistrusting idiot. He'd thrown away the best thing to ever happen to him and still wasn't smart enough to realize it yet. He'd known Conner for years, first through his brother and then later through those stupid trips the guys had taken together. Hell, Conner had even been the one to introduce Larissa and Jason.

Her thoughts, and the accompanying tension pounding through her spine, were so painfully familiar, Larissa wanted to cry.

Holy crap, it was like being sent back in a time machine. Larissa pressed two fingers to her temple, trying to stem the throbbing vein. Crazy. Anything she had with Jason was in the past. She'd be damned if she'd let him know how much seeing him still hurt. Or give him any idea how devastated she'd been when he'd left her.

Cool, calm and collected. Yep, that was her.

"So why are you here again?" she asked, silently reciting her new mantra.

"I'm here to see the Cartright brothers about a business deal." He raised a brow. "And you? Waiting for a date?"

"What?" She ignored the date dig. Jason was here about the storefront? That was impossible. "This is a joke, right? You can't be interested in the available retail space. You're too busy chasing your childhood, running all over the planet looking for new ways to risk your life."

"Aww, you know me so well," Jason replied as he made a show of slouching against the wall, while giving her a look so intense, she glanced down to make sure her jacket was buttoned and her boobs weren't hanging out. "But despite that deep insight into my character, it's actually true. I'm opening a store here at the Cartright."

"You mean *you'd like* to open a store. There's only one space available and I'm pretty sure Conner and company will be giving it to me," Larissa answered, trying to sound cocky. Then, seeing the fake affable look on his face slip a little, she shook her head quickly before he could make some snotty guy remark about how she'd convinced Conner to give her the space. "Why would you need a storefront, anyway? Don't you have mountains to climb?"

"Not getting much climbing satisfaction these days, huh?"

Larissa tilted her head to the side and gave him a long once-over. "Oh, believe me, I've never climbed mountains as satisfying as the one I'm scaling now."

Even more satisfying was watching that lie take the shine off his cocky smile.

"Is that a fact?"

Larissa gave a little shrug, then brushing an imaginary bit of lint off her black pencil skirt, used the brief pause to try and catch her breath. She never lied well, and given the dearth of mountains in her current love life, she wasn't too sure she could pull it off now.

"Excuse me," Conner said from the doorway. Larissa and Jason both turned. Larissa with a grateful look at the intervention, Jason with a glare. Conner's friendly smile didn't waver. "Perhaps you can delay the rest of this reunion?

The committee is on its way out but wanted a chance to talk with the two of you first, if you don't mind."

Larissa swept up her briefcase and with a quick tug at the hem of her black silk ruffled jacket, hurried toward the door. She slowed her rush when she realized she'd have to brush past Jason to get to the freedom on the other side.

Jason and his magic dick. Larissa lifted her chin and pretended she didn't feel its lure. Skirting carefully around him, she gave Conner a quick, grateful smile.

She also pretended she didn't hear Jason's low growl.

Knowing she should be focused on the committee, Larissa attempted to quickly sort through her tangled feelings. Why did Jason have to come back? What the hell did he need with a store? And why was he still so gorgeous? Shouldn't there be a rule for heartbreakers? That they were punished with a double chin or ten pounds for every year of misery they caused?

"Ms. Zahn? Conner was just filling us in on a few details. I didn't realize you and Mr. Cantrell knew each other," Ben said, breaking into her reverie.

"Quite well, as a matter of fact," Jason added, his voice still that same husky tone she heard so often in her dreams.

"Hardly at all, really," she dismissed just as quickly. "We met through Conner, actually. All things considered, I'd say Jason was practically a stranger."

A blatant lie. The room was lit up from the sparks flying between the two of them. She couldn't be the only one feeling it.

Conner, who should have seen the direction this was heading, steepled his fingers together and watched her with an enigmatic look. Jason just grinned, that devilish dimple flashing.

"Oh, I wouldn't say we were strangers, Larissa. Not after all we've been through together."

Conner smirked. The men on either side of him sat up a little straighter. They obviously sensed the vibes.

But Larissa's Romance Rule number three—learned the hard way—insisted that there be no airing of dirty laundry in public. It always, absolutely always, came back to bite you in the butt.

"So how long has it been since the two of you saw each other?" the pen-tapper asked.

"One year, eight months. Give or take a few days," Jason said, his tone so off-hand that it took Larissa a few beats to realize what he'd said. After a mental finger count, she realized he was exactly right.

Larissa had a smile on her face before she realized her lips had moved. He responded with a smile of his own, his gaze sweeping her body with a look so warm, she knew he was remembering her naked. Color washed over her cheeks and she gave herself a mental head slap. Proof positive why Jason was so bad for her. His sweet little comments made her feel like she was the most important person in his world. Right up until she remembered that she barely made his top ten list.

Which, she reminded herself as her own smile fell away, was just one of the reasons why he was so bad for her.

"Did the two of you go to school together?" Ben asked, his chubby face alight with curiosity. Larissa didn't know why he was so curious. It had nothing to do with either of their abilities to launch a store. But she answered anyway.

"No. I went to the local schools and Jason traveled."

"My parents were archaeologists," Jason interjected. "I was homeschooled on the road."

"But you hung out together? You had the same friends?"

"I used to hang out with Conner," Larissa said, her tone syrup-sweet. There went Jason's smile. "Jason's brother and Conner's were college roommates. Jason and I met at some party the Cartrights threw."

"Then what all is the *all* that you've been through together?" the irritating guy with the pen prodded, referring to Jason's earlier taunt.

They both ignored him. Larissa out of respect for the dirty laundry rule. Jason, she was sure, because he never answered anything that didn't suit him.

"I take it the two of you didn't realize you were competing for the same space?" Ben asked.

"No. It's been a couple years since Larissa and I had time to catch up, so this is a big surprise," Jason replied.

He shot Conner a look. Larissa couldn't believe everyone wasn't seeing through Jason's mellow demeanor. There was anger, impatience and a hint of worry in that blue-eyed glare. She understood the first two, but the latter? What did Jason have to worry about?

"And now that you know you both want the same thing?" Pen-tapper gave a sharklike grin, looking like the kind of guy who plunked down money to watch any form of violent sports. "Are you both still interested? Or is this one of those situations where you both say you want it, then after we spend hours assessing the situation and what's best for the hotel, one of you gets all sappy and backs down so the other doesn't get his or her panties in a twist?"

"Franklin!" Conner snapped.

"Hey, I think we have the right to know. We need to make a decision and I don't see much point in wasting time debating if one of them is going to step aside for the other."

His words ended in a buzz as the room did a little spin around Larissa's head. Both still interested? So Jason actually did want the store space? Why? For what? Did that mean he was really back to stay? She wasn't sure what panicked her more. The idea of battling against him for her dream space. Or knowing he was living in the same town again. It was hard enough to forget him when he was traipsing around the world. It'd be impossible to put him out of her mind if he was within touching distance.

But maybe, just maybe, she'd get the space…and he'd go away again. A girl could hope, right?

"Mr. Franklin, despite the tone of your questions, I do believe you have a good point. You're concerned with both your own time and what's best for the hotel," Larissa acknowledged.

She was proud of herself for sounding so reasonable when she wanted to smack all four men over the head with her purse. Conner for getting her into this, Franklin for being a jerk. Jason for all the memories and regrets beating through her. And Ben? Well, he was a guy and at this particular moment, they were obviously all on the same side.

"But you don't have anything to worry about," Jason interjected, obviously knowing exactly what she'd been about to say. "Despite our history, Larissa is right. She and I are practically strangers now. I want this space too much to let it go for old time's sake. And I'm sure she feels the same."

"Then you might be willing to negotiate?"

Larissa's stomach took a dive. Negotiate what? Rent? She could barely afford the amount Conner had told her. The promotional deal? The marketing tie-in with the hotel was the only reason she could justify the rent she could barely afford. What else could be negotiated?

"No," Jason said firmly. He didn't even look at her, instead keeping his gaze on Franklin. He still looked as kick-back friendly as always. He was leaning against the window ledge, one foot crossed over the other and his hands in the front pockets of his jeans. He even had a friendly half smile on his face. But his eyes were hard, his jaw set. He wasn't taking any crap.

He flicked a quick glance her way. In that second, she realized he wasn't letting these guys give her any crap, either. She swallowed, warmth filling her heart.

"The terms were already presented and we agreed to them," Jason continued. "The decision is yours to make, of course. But neither of us will undercut or undermine the other so you can take advantage of the situation."

"No," Conner said before either of the other men could respond. "First of all, that's not how we do business at Cartright. And second, while the decision on which business will occupy the space is up to my associates, all terms and conditions are mine to make."

He stood, his associates reluctantly getting to their feet as well. Obviously, Ben had totally forgotten about his impending flight. "We'll discuss the situation, and I'll get you both the decision by tomorrow. But for now, I have a dinner appointment to get to. So we're going to take a look at the display while you both finish things up here."

Larissa gave a small shrug. Finish? She and Jason had finished a long time ago. Two years ago, in fact, when he'd taken his engagement ring and walked away.

THE SHOCK OF SEEING Larissa was starting to fade. The in-your-face lust seeing her always inspired was still flaming hot and strong, but years of adventures had taught Jason the wisdom in avoiding the kind of danger that led to certain doom.

And Larissa and him? Yep, definitely doomed.

"Wait, I'd like to see the storefront, too," he called out. He had no idea why. He didn't give a rat's ass what the store looked like. He didn't plan to spend any time in it. That was Peter's chore. But Larissa had seen it. Hell, she'd set up a display in it, apparently. So he'd better at least pretend he cared if he wanted to make a good impression.

"To be fair, why don't you give us five minutes to look over the display, then come on down," the guy named Ben suggested with a covetous look at Larissa.

Jason narrowed his eyes. Did this loser think by voting in her favor, he'd have a shot at making time with Larissa? She might have rotten taste in men, himself excluded, but she would never go out with a guy for a store space.

Jason eyed the pudgy guy's friendly face. Unless she was attracted to him?

Was that jealousy stabbing him in the gut?

Nah. He had no reason to be jealous. No rights where Larissa was concerned. They were over. Long over. So no, that couldn't be jealousy.

The green haze in his eyes said differently.

"The main hotel doors are all programmed to lock automatically. Because we're not open yet, we haven't brought in security guards so don't be surprised if you don't run into anyone. Feel free to explore as long as you like," Conner informed them. "Jason, if you'll give us a few minutes, you're welcome to stay behind and look around after we've gone. Larissa has the key to the store itself. I trust you'll lock it up and make sure things are secure before you leave."

"Sure. Yeah, I can do that. I'd love to look around," Jason lied. What the hell was there to look at? None of the stores were open. Hell, Daniel said they hadn't even brought in fixtures or inventory yet. Besides, unless the building was filled with potential clients, he wouldn't have a clue what he was checking out.

"I'll wait in here, too, if you don't mind," Larissa said. "I'd rather you get the full effect of the display and feel comfortable to honestly discuss it among yourselves. I'll go down after you've finished and gather up the materials, if that's okay?"

Ahh, there it was. His reason for waiting. Not because he wanted to spend more time with Larissa, although, man, was she looking hot. Her hair, that riotous mass of glossy black curls, was styled in a way that framed her face and accented those huge eyes. And that body? He shifted uncomfortably to ease the tightening denim. Smoking hot. Her skirt hugged her hips and was way too long, hitting her just below the knees and hiding legs he remembered as deliciously sleek. But the fabric cupped her butt just right. And her ruffled jacket looked soft and inviting, despite the long sleeves and lack of cleavage displayed.

But just because she looked great didn't mean he was hanging out to spend time with her. Nope, smart men didn't have to fall off the same cliff twice to know it was going to hurt.

They did, however, carefully assess the competition, looking for information and weaknesses that would let them win the game.

So. He was assessing. That's all.

"Thanks to both of you for coming in for the presentations. We appreciate it. And we'll let you know right away," Conner said, stopping in the doorway to give Larissa a quick hug. It was all Jason could do not to dive across the room and rip the guy's hands off of her. When they'd made their peace last year, Conner had claimed that even though he'd hoped for more, he and Larissa had only ever been friends. But maybe he'd lied?

Or maybe things had changed since then.

And maybe, Jason reminded himself with clenched teeth, it was none of his business anymore.

On his way out the door after Conner, Franklin gave Larissa a stiff smile, then shook Jason's hand encouragingly.

Ben looked like he wanted to drool all over her feet. He gave Jason a quick look, noted the scowl, and offered her his hand instead.

Smart man.

She might not be Jason's any longer, but he was pretty sure he'd have to beat the hell out of any guy who hit on her in front of him.

It was like a reflex or instinct or something. Totally unplanned and, well, realistically? Unwelcomed. Because he knew from painful experience that the last thing Larissa wanted was anything to do with his...what had she called it? Oh yeah, his pathetic, half-assed commitment-phobic posturing.

He'd asked her to marry him, hadn't he? So how could he be commitment-phobic? Which meant the rest of her accusations were equally unfounded and ridiculous.

Too bad she looked so damned good, though. She'd always been a cute kid. Tiny, like a fairy, with masses of black curls and brown eyes too big for her angular face. Her diminutive size and quiet nature had kept her off Jason's radar the first couple times they'd met. Hell, she'd still been in high school then. Way off-limits.

But her first summer home from college? Well, Jason Cantrell might be a little slow on the uptake sometimes, but he made up for it with enthusiasm. He'd taken one look at her golden legs in little cutoff shorts and he'd fallen hard and fast. Which pretty well described their entire courtship and, he was ashamed to admit, their first time in bed together.

She'd broken his heart.

And now she wanted to ruin his brilliant business plan. Nope. Not gonna happen.

"So," he said slowly, leaning against the table and trying to look relaxed as he took a long, appreciative look at the woman fidgeting by the door.

"So?"

So, how was she doing?

So, what'd happened between her and Conner over the years?

So, why did she want to set up shop here, in a hotel?

So, when had she quit working for that old guy at the bookstore and what had she been doing since then?

"So, are you still single?" He winced as he heard the words, which had been nowhere on his list of approved questions.

From the look she gave him, it wasn't on her list, either.

"I can't believe you're interested in opening a store," she said, ignoring his question. "Are you leaving Can-Do Adventures?"

"Nope. Can-Do is doing great. We're in twenty-three countries now, touring every continent."

Her smile was fast and warm. You had to hand it to Larissa, she might hold grudges and have all sorts of insane ideas about relationships. But the woman was as sweet as they came, always ready to celebrate someone else's success and happiness.

"You're living the dream," she murmured, using his oft-repeated goal, as she gathered folders and diagrams to shove in her big leather bag. "Peter must be thrilled, too. I hope he's well."

Jason narrowed his eyes, trying to see if she was being sarcastic. Larissa had always had a subtle hand with the snark. But she looked genuine. Amazing, considering his brother had done everything he could to break the two of them up.

"He's as well as can be expected," he said with a shrug.

"Is something wrong?" Her words were politely concerned, but this time he saw the look of naughty glee in her eyes. Like she was imagining Peter stewing in a cannibal's cauldron.

"Yeah. He's been ordered to quit traveling. It won't be the same without him."

"I'm so sorry. Will he be okay?" she asked, stepping forward to put a consoling hand on his arm. Jason's body reacted like she'd rubbed up against him wearing only black stockings and a feather boa. Hard, hot and horny in an instant.

"He's terminal," Jason said, barely aware of his words as he tossed off the term he'd often used to razz his brother.

She blanched. Her fingers curled into his forearm, short nails biting the flesh. Jason's dick hardened even more as he flashed back to a memory of those same nails digging into his shoulder as he thrust into her welcoming body.

"Oh, Jason. I'm so sorry. Your parents must be heart-broken."

"Nah, Mom likes Meghan."

"Meghan?" She frowned. "What?"

Jason did a quick rewind and realized what she must have thought.

"Peter's getting married. It's a terminal case of commit-ment," he explained quickly, trying not to grin.

She pulled her hand away like he was covered in some-thing gross. The disgusted look on her face echoed the action.

"You're impossible."

"Nope, sweetheart. How could you forget? I'm incredibly easy. At least, where you were concerned."

She didn't smile this time, but her cheeks turned a cute shade of pink. She made a show of looking at her watch.

"I think the committee should be finished with the store-front by now. I'm going to gather my display."

She turned away, bending to pick up a sleek-looking black

leather briefcase with red piping to match the shoes she was wearing. His eyes lingered on her feet, remembering the amazing torment she'd been able to give him with those toes. Was she wearing polish? He'd bet she was, something intense and sexy like red.

He wanted to find out almost as much as he wanted that store space.

"I'll go with you."

"You don't have to."

"Sure I do. You know where it is and you have the key," he reminded her.

"Fine," she said with a shrug. "You can use the time to explain why you're really here."

He could tell she was trying to look like she didn't care. But she was strangling that leather handle, so he figured he was bugging her.

Good. She was bugging him, too.

She headed for the door. Jason grabbed the koteka case he'd brought in as part of his pitch. He frowned at the long, worn cardboard of the dusty box. "I never got to show them my penis."

Well, that got her attention. Larissa turned to stare, choking back a laugh. "Literally? Or figuratively?"

"Both." He held up the box in an unspoken offer to show her. She gave him a long, considering look and shook her head. Guess she wasn't willing to see his figurative or literal penis.

"It's a koteka," he explained, stepping up to match his stride to hers as she headed down the hallway toward the elevators. "A penis sheath, actually. I brought it back from Papua New Guinea. It's been blessed by a medicine man and is supposed to impart virility and sexual prowess on the man who wears it."

"I thought you boys had little blue pills for that now," she said, stepping into the elevator and waiting until he'd joined her before punching the button for the lobby.

"The natives are a little behind in their pharmacology. Besides, this is better. It's magic."

"A magic dick, huh?" He didn't understand the amusement on her face, but loved the sound of Larissa's laugh as it bubbled out, bouncing off the stainless steel walls. Her look invited him to entertain her. He loved that look. He figured that was why she was so into books. She had that childlike quality of suspending disbelief and giving a story her undivided attention. He remembered a couple trips, he'd listened to the local's tales, then hurried back to his tent to write down the details so he could see that same look when he told his latest adventure story.

"Magic?" she prodded, her lips curved and her brow arched.

"The medicine man promised that the man who possesses this koteka will not only be sexually blessed, but that he'd have lifelong happiness with the woman he pleasured."

"Nice," she said with a sigh. Then she shook her head, as if she was refusing to fall under his spell. "But what does that have to do with the Cartright Hotel and its boutiques?"

"This hotel is a couples' gig, right? So I figured we'd showcase Can-Do with a museum of sorts. I've collected fertility figures and tools from all over the world. What better way to get the hotel patrons in the mood."

"You want to set up a sex shop for world travelers?"

"Ha. No. I want to set up a physical storefront for Can-Do. Something to lure travelers in via the hotel and the promotion Cartright promises. Along with some exclusive adventures found only through Cartright, I figure sex is the best way to entice people in to take a look."

"Leave it to you to reduce the wonders of traveling the

world down to sex," she muttered with a dismissive roll of her eyes.

"Haven't you heard? Sex sells, sweetheart."

And damned if Jason didn't have some he'd like to sell her.

# 4

BEFORE LARISSA DID MORE than blink, Jason shifted. He slapped his hands against the steel wall of the elevator, one on either side of her head. Larissa gave a squeaky little yelp. When had he gotten so fast?

She sucked in a breath. Her brain warned her to push him away. Her heart warned her to remember how badly he'd hurt her. Her body babbled hubba-da-hubba.

She almost looked down to make sure she hadn't melted into a puddle at his feet. He'd always affected her like this. Long before he'd had a clue, in fact.

He was clued in now, though.

His gaze swept over her heated cheeks, resting briefly on her lips before drifting slowly down, like a gentle caress, to her chest. The intensity of his look made Larissa want to look down and make sure her silk jacket was still closed sedately, hiding her red satin camisole.

The soft layers of fabric couldn't hide her body's reaction, though. She knew from the aching heaviness of her breasts that her nipples were in stand-up-and-pay-attention mode.

Just the way he liked them.

Jason's blue eyes glinted with a naughty sort of satisfaction when they met hers. His glance said he was amused, horny and hell-bent on pushing her to step up and meet his sexual challenge.

"So, are you in the market?" he asked, his words low and husky.

Her mouth watered. She swallowed, then had to swallow again before asking, "Market?"

"For sex."

Her thighs melted from the heat his words inspired. Her breath sped up and it was all she could do not to wrap her leg around his waist and press herself against his hard body.

"I'm not really in the mood for shopping," she lied.

"I'll bet I can change your mind."

She'd bet he could, too.

That was the problem with Jason. When he got this close, he made her want to throw away all her inhibitions—and her underwear—and give in to anything he asked.

When she was with him, she forgot what was important. She let go of her dreams. Her hopes for the life she'd grown up wishing for and never having. With Jason, she tossed aside the things she valued, like a stable home and family. Like romance and a career she loved. Like believing that she could be—deserved to be—the most important thing in someone's life. Important enough that he wanted to spend his life, all of it, not just random weekdays when he wasn't off having fun, with her.

Which meant she had to make sure he didn't get this close, she warned herself. With that in mind, she hauled out her fake smile again—oh, boy was it getting a lot of use today—and, steeling herself, pressed her hand against his chest.

Her fingers wanted to curl into the hard, warm flesh. Her palm tingled when it felt the soft dusting of hair there, where the top button gave way to the V-neck.

She forced herself to push him away, though.

"I've already sampled what you're selling," she reminded him. "And I'm afraid it's not worth the price."

Jason's eyes narrowed. He stood rock firm against her hand, not moving an inch.

Larissa's heart raced. Her throat dried. Had she gone too far? All of a sudden, she was vividly aware that she was alone with him. Not just in this elevator, but probably in the entire building. He was bigger than she was. Stronger and in every way, more powerful. She wasn't afraid he'd hurt her. At least, not her body.

But she was terrified that if she let him, he'd break her heart. Again.

Then his face relaxed. Underneath her palm, she felt the tension ease in his body. He gave her a quick smile, then with a one-shouldered shrug, moved back.

Her body chilled without the heat of his. She curled her fingers into her palm to ease the ache.

"You're missing out," he promised, assuming his usual pose by leaning back against the opposite wall of the elevator.

"Sex, sex, sex," Larissa groused, trying to sound like she hadn't just had a mental orgasm. "What is it with guys and sex today?"

"You mean I'm not your first?" he teased.

She pressed her lips together to hold back a smile. You had to hand it to him. Jason never copped an attitude when he was rejected. He just took it in stride.

Not that she'd rejected him often. At least, not in the beginning. From the moment Jason noticed she was female, all he'd had to do was give her a sexy look from those intense blue eyes and she'd dropped anything and everything. Including her pants.

Until the end.

Her shoulders drooped with the weight of the memory.

It was the end she had to keep in mind, here. That was real. The rest? Like all of Jason's adventures, the rest of their relationship had been a temporary fantasy.

"You're not even my first this hour," she finally answered, thinking of the pen-tapper and his desire for her to sex up her store plans. It was the truth, and thankfully let her side-step the humiliation of admitting that she hadn't had a guy talk sex with her in over three months. Unless she counted that one bookstore customer who'd asked for a reference book on the health effects of Viagra. And she really didn't want to count him.

"The last hour?" he repeated. His words were measured, like he was weighing them carefully. "You and Conner had a little tryst before the meeting?"

"I didn't think you even knew what a tryst was," she quipped with a stiff smile as her stomach gave a little dip.

She gave Jason a careful look. She'd forgotten how jealous he got. At first, she'd thought it was kinda cute. Like he thought she was so gorgeous, he couldn't trust men around her. But then she'd realized that his jealousy meant he didn't trust her, either.

And as they'd found out, they couldn't have a relationship without trust.

Thankfully, the elevator reached the lobby so she could escape.

"The stores are over this way," she said, waving her hand toward the marble archway on the left that led to the boutiques. Their steps echoed loudly on the polished wood floors as they walked around a large statue of a naked couple entwined in a never-ending embrace. "That closed-in archway on the right will lead to the hotel's lobby and registration area when construction is finished. Conner took me through before he locked the doors. It's lovely."

"Lovely enough to justify the rent on the storefront?"

She slanted him a look. Neither of them had grown up with the wealth that Conner had, but they hadn't been poor, either. In the past, Jason's attitude toward money had always been "easy come, easy go." When had he started worrying about cost-effectiveness?

"I'm not an expert, but based on the other Cartright holdings and the luxury of the areas I toured, this will be a four-star hotel."

They stepped through the archway and into the long marble hall lined with upscale boutiques on both sides and planters overflowing with lush flowers, cushioned benches and romantic statuary in the center.

"Between the clientele, the caliber of the other stores already renting space here and the incredible promotion package Cartright is offering, the rent is a steal," she added as they passed stores that, while empty, displayed well-known names. Tiffany's, La Perla, MAC. "From what I understand, there's a waiting list for storefront openings. The only reason we're even being considered is that Conner wanted to bring in local merchants."

Why the hell was she trying to convince her competition of the worthiness of the prize?

"It sounds like you've done your homework" was all he said, though.

Stopping between a shop with a sign promising Godiva Chocolates and the storefront where she'd set up her display, she studied Jason's face. Why did he really want this space? It wasn't his style, nor would it lend itself to his business.

So what was he up to?

Before she could ask, he stepped forward to get the full effect of the window display she'd set up. Conner had left the doors open in welcome, and even though the space was virtually empty beyond that door, the effect was still warm and welcoming.

And, she thought with a soft sigh as she eyed the display, so very romantic. A pair of high-heeled ladies slippers were tucked alongside a stack of romance novels, topped with an antique blown glass perfume atomizer. A bouquet of roses tumbled in colorful profusion from a sterling silver vase and a handful of DVDs were splayed, like magazines, just beneath it.

From where they were standing, the display Larissa had set up on the checkout counter beckoned them, like a little finger wave, into the store. She knew she couldn't compete with Godiva, so she'd gone for the healthier romance treats. A cut glass bowl of strawberries, a bottle of champagne and an array of imported cheeses and crackers, all still in their wrappers. The effect, along with the rest of the merchandise, made her think of a romantic weekend tryst.

She just hoped it'd make Conner's partners think that way, too. Larissa nibbled on her thumbnail, nerves dancing up and down her spine again as she squinted, wondering if she should have left the ivory cashmere throw on the counter instead of moving it to the settee.

"Wow. This is…" Jason trailed off, taking a step back and crossing his arms over his chest to stare at the display in the window. "This is great. It's definitely not what I expected."

"You expected my display to suck?" she asked, giving him a frown.

Did it suck? Her eyes sped from item to item. Maybe she should have used her cell phone to take a picture and send to Chloe for a second opinion before she'd told the partners it was finished.

"No. I expect everything you do to be great," Jason said, interrupting her neurotic obsessing. His words were so off-hand she knew he really meant them. Her shoulders softened. She wished she had half the faith in herself that he'd always shown.

Argh. Larissa's hands were halfway to her hair to tug at the curls. It was only the very real fear that if she did, her hair would frizz out and she'd look like Bozo the clown that kept her from grabbing hold and pulling.

She had to stop this. Every time Jason said something sweet, or gave her one of those sexy looks of his, she melted. Her mind was so filled with images of wrapping herself around his naked body that she forgot all the reasons why they'd split up.

He was bad for her. Like a chocolate fountain and bowl of strawberries were to a sugar addict, he was pure temptation. A temptation she needed to resist at all costs.

"I'm going to pack up," she muttered, hurrying through the mostly empty store toward the back room where she'd stashed her box. The sooner she got away from him, the better. First she had to go home. Then she had to call Conner and make sure she got this space. She'd even date Ben or add the sexy merchandise Franklin wanted if it meant she could seal the deal.

Not just because she wanted the space, although she did, so, so badly. She'd do anything—everything—in her power to make sure Jason didn't move back to town.

She had to.

AMUSED AT HOW FLUSTERED Larissa seemed, Jason sauntered along behind her. He poked at a candle, flicked a crystal teardrop on the wall sconce. Even though he knew it was rude, he smirked a little.

She'd practically melted at his feet in that elevator. Now she was rushing around like the devil was chasing her. Since he knew who she'd consigned horns, he figured he might as well enjoy the role.

"What are you doing here, a sort of general store? I thought you'd have a bookstore, to tell you the truth. I mean, you read incessantly," he called to her, as she scurried through a doorway in the back of the store. "Hell, you could have turned your apartment into a bookstore, what with every wall a bookcase and the stacks teetering on the floors and tables."

"It'll be a bookstore," she said as she came back into the room with a cardboard box held in her arms like a shield between them. "It'll just stock other things, too."

Jason frowned at the defensive note in her voice. What was up with that? He looked around, trying to see what it was about this stuff that'd embarrass her. He picked up a candle in a frosted glass jar, giving it a sniff. Nice. Flowery but not nauseating. He rubbed his fingers over a soft, fluffy blanket she'd thrown on the couch. Books, DVDs and CDs were stacked everywhere, along with some pretty statues and other girly things.

So, what was the problem?

"Is this a secondary location you're hoping to open here?" he probed.

"No."

His frown turned into a scowl. She'd already started planning for her bookstore when they'd been engaged. So what'd happened? Had it failed? Was that why she was so touchy?

"So, what've you been doing if not running your own store?"

"Working, of course." She shifted, her hair falling in a cloud of curls to hide her face. But he'd seen the color on her cheeks.

He narrowed his eyes.

"Working where?"

"At the bookstore, not that it's any of your business." Her chilly tone was at odds with the heat he could almost feel radiating off her face. It only took him a second to figure out why.

Shock zapped through Jason like a lightning bolt. She'd been so big on following her dream and had tried to lure him into that dreaming of the future thing, too. For a little while, he'd actually believed they could make things work, even though he'd known better. Half the reason they'd broken up was her need to be landlocked to a bookstore she swore would take all of her attention to make a success.

Well, maybe that was the half of the reason he hadn't told her. He was pretty sure she'd say the entire reason they'd broken up was that he was an insecure commitment-phobic asshole who couldn't make the long haul.

But they were focusing on her issues. Not his.

"You're still at old man Murphy's, aren't you? Working his bookstore? Same place you've been since high school?" he growled. "You never went out on your own? You never opened your own store? You're kidding, right?"

She'd always wanted to open her own bookstore. She'd always known that while her aunt loved her, the older woman had planned to leave her estate to her beloved cat charities. And Larissa was fine with that. She'd been determined to make her own way. She'd saved for years, stocking away part of her income and all of the insurance money she'd gotten when her parents had died. Having her own business was all she'd ever talked about.

He stared at the top of her forehead, the only part of her face he could see through the cloud of hair. She ignored him as she carefully wrapped a heart-shaped crystal dish in bubble wrap, then in paper.

Jason wanted to demand that she explain herself. He wanted to know why she hadn't grabbed her dreams before this.

But…what was the point?

They'd finished years ago. And just as soon as she got her stuff packed up, they'd be finished again.

He ignored the burning in his gut at that thought and shoved his hands into his pockets.

"Look, I've got things to do. You have Conner's keys with you, right? You can lock up after you've finished gathering your stuff."

Her head came up so fast, her hair practically floated around her shoulders. Brown eyes widened. Pale, full lips parted, then she pressed them tight together and sighed. Probably in relief.

"That's a great idea."

The overhead lights flickered. Jason glanced into the open space, then up at the skylight centered over the hotel's mini-mall. No storm. He stepped out of the store and looked up and down the bank of stores.

Weird.

The lights flared bright. Then the entire mall dove into blackness.

"What the hell…"

The loud crash of metal hitting marble screeched through the mall as the security bars slammed down to close off the entrance between the mall and the hotel.

Larissa screamed and jumped toward him, her hand clutching his arm. It was only instinct, he was sure. Still, he wrapped one arm around her shoulder to reassure her.

And to keep her from stomping on his toes with those killer heels of hers.

The darkness wrapped around them, terrifyingly heavy and dense. For just a second, she leaned into him. He felt her softly tremble. He loved the feel of having her in his arms again. Jason closed his eyes, reveling in her delicious scent. Before he could pull her closer, she stepped away and wrapped her arms around herself.

He had no reason to feel hurt. He wouldn't be upset if a woman he'd just met didn't want him giving her a comfort hug, would he? And Larissa had said it herself earlier. They were practically strangers.

His eyes started to adjust to the change in light. Which meant Larissa's were, too. Needing to hide the pathetically bereft look on his face, he strode over to a wall by the entrance to the store and flipped the light switch a couple times.

Nothing.

"Looks like the power's out," he said needlessly.

"What do you think happened?" she asked.

He could tell she was trying to sound calm, but there was a layer of panic in Larissa's voice. Why? She wasn't claustrophobic, so why was she so freaked about being stuck in here?

Or was it the company she was freaked about? Despite his irritation, he grinned. It was gratifying to know he still had such an effect on her. Especially since she seemed so determined to ignore her effect on him. He hadn't exactly been a monk in the last few years, but it'd been a long time since he'd made a woman nervous. Most of the gals he spent time with, in and out of bed, were a little harder, a little cooler. They knew the score and liked to play.

Then again, as he recalled, Larissa was pretty good with the game playing. Even with his ring on her finger, she'd kept her fingers in the dating pool. Peter had warned him that no pretty girl would sit around at home reading a book while her guy was off playing in the jungle. And hey, big brother had been right. Jason had come home from a trip and she'd been off yachting for the weekend. When he'd accused her of getting too friendly with Conner, a guy who they both knew damned well had a thing for her, she'd refused to deny it. Instead, she'd tossed his ring back in his face.

Gut burning, Jason tried to shake off the bitterness of the past. He needed to get out of here. Being around Larissa, all the memories and the temptation, felt like a punch to the gut.

"Maybe the electricity is on an automatic timer or something," he mused, looking around. "Don't worry about it. There's still enough light coming through the skylight for you to pack up, right?"

"Right," she murmured. "I'll hurry up and finish."

Neither of them mentioned his earlier intention to leave her to pack up alone. They both knew he wouldn't abandon her now. No longer carefully wrapping each item in packing paper, she started stacking things in the boxes as quickly as possible.

Jason strode over to the automatic doors that led from the boutique to a parking area. The doors didn't slide open when he stepped in front of them.

A tiny tendril of panic started winding its way through his gut. Maybe there wasn't an automatic timer. Jason's gaze shifted beyond the doors and his stomach sank.

"Shit," he muttered, staring out the heavy, brass-framed glass.

"What?" Larissa called, the concern in her voice rising to match the concern in his.

The hotel was high atop a hill, with a gorgeous bird's-eye view. The front of the building, he knew, was landscaped with large trees and flowering bushes, giving it the feel of a secluded oasis. But this side was still under construction.

Jason surveyed the cityscape. It looked deserted, bereft of all life. No color, no movement. Just…blackness. Other than the pale pinkish-orange of the setting sun, there wasn't a light to be seen.

He grabbed the keys and went through them until he found one that fit. He wiggled the key, then shook the door again. He narrowed his eyes, noting the solid steel bolts coming from the top and bottom of the door into the floor and ceiling. He shook the door again. The bolts held firm.

Shit.

"Jason?"

He rested his head briefly against the cool glass, wondering what he'd done to piss off Fate so much. Then, with a deep breath, he turned to face his ex-fiancée.

"So there's good news and bad news," he told her.

"The good?"

"The hotel and boutiques aren't on a timer."

She frowned, her gaze shifting over his shoulder to the view of the city. Horror widened her eyes as they met his again.

"Yeah, that's the bad. It looks like it's a city-wide blackout. Conner will be pleased to know his security measures work. The doors must've bolted shut when the power went off."

She shook her head, holding that soft fluffy blanket against her chest.

"You have a cell phone?" he asked, trying to remember Conner's number.

"I left mine in the car," she confessed. Through the faint light from the glass doors he could see her nibbling at the soft temptation of her bottom lip. Jason almost groaned. "Do you have one?" she asked.

"Dead."

"But there must be phones in the mall?" she said, looking around desperately.

"On the other side of the security bars," he remembered. "Nothing in here, though. Daniel said all the stores would be responsible for their own."

"We're stuck?" she asked, sounding like they were doomed.

"Yep."

Doomed might be right. Jason had climbed Mt. Everest in a snowstorm. He'd led a group of Girl Scouts out of the rainforest after an earthquake. He'd broken up a fight in a sleazy bar in Taiwan. But he'd never been this out of his element.

They had no supplies. He hadn't thought to bring a backpack and field rations to a business meeting. And he doubted, for all its professed powers, that the penis he had in that box was going to be of much help in this situation.

They had no means of communication. It was Friday night and the building was empty. Surely someone would miss them eventually. Conner would probably meet them in the morning to pick up the keys. But that was tomorrow.

At least they had shelter. Maybe there was a vending machine or something around for food. But Larissa had pretty much called it.

They were trapped.

Just the two of them. And the tempting softness of that blanket.

Jason had no idea what possessed him. He knew better. Hell, hadn't he lectured himself once already today? But... The devil made him do it, as his mother always said.

He gently pried the blanket from Larissa's fingers. Holding the whisper-soft fabric in one hand, he swept it around her shoulders, fisting both sides together to trap her in the cloudy white material.

"Guess we'll be spending tonight together, hmm." He leaned closer, his lips a hairbreadth from hers and asked, "What do you think we should do to pass the time?"

# 5

LARISSA KNEW EXACTLY what she was going to do to pass the time until they got out of here.

She was going to panic.

To avoid letting Jason know how freaked out she was and lose any semblance of control, she'd do it quietly. But she'd definitely be doing it.

She could already feel the mean fingers of anxiety grabbing at her, twisting her stomach in knots and making her woozy.

She couldn't be locked in. She had too much to do. She needed to call Conner and pitch her idea one more time. She had a column due Monday that she'd put aside this evening to write. She'd left spaghetti sauce out on the counter, defrosting. Being stuck here wasn't an option.

Especially not with Jason. He was kryptonite to her superhero. Chocolate éclairs to her diet. Tequila to her temperance vow. He was everything that tempted her. Every indulgence she secretly wished for, even though she knew he was so bad for her.

And her willpower to hold out against a temptation like him was limited, at best. She'd have been able to wave goodbye if they walked out now. She was sure of it. But after being trapped together? She'd mentally unzipped his pants with her teeth the minute she'd seen him. If they were stuck together, how long would her willpower last?

As if her internal struggle was written across her face, Jason smiled. His hands tightened on the blanket. The warmth of his fingers, where they brushed the delicate fabric of her jacket just over her breasts, seeped into her skin.

Her flesh warmed. Her vision blurred. Her head did a couple spins, like a carnival ride.

"Maybe we should—"

"We should find a way out," she blurted. She tried to hide the breathlessness of her words by shifting, tugging the soft fabric of the blanket from his hands. She stepped backward so fast her cute red heels slipped on the marble floor. She windmilled, trying to regain balance.

Jason grabbed both of her arms, keeping her from sliding across the floor on her butt.

"Falling at my feet?" he teased.

"Lucky for me, you keep saving me from that humiliation," she retorted, her cheeks on fire. She made sure she was steady, then quickly, but carefully, stepped away.

"You okay?"

"I'm fine," she said, tugging her jacket into place. Then with reluctant courtesy, she gave him a look from under her lashes and murmured, "Thank you."

"Sure. Can't have you getting hurt. It's not like we can call for help, and as much as I'd love to play doctor with you, I don't have a first aid kit handy."

Larissa's lips twitched. Then she remembered, she was immune to his charm.

"We're really stuck?" she asked, hoping he'd tell her he had some clever escape planned.

"Until the power comes back on. Or until tomorrow at the latest," he said instead.

Locked in, all night, with Jason? Larissa's heart thudded against her chest. "What about a security guard? Or Peter? Won't he be looking for you?"

Jason shook his head. "Nah. Remember what Conner said? They don't have a security team in place yet. Conner figured the locks would be enough for now. And now that Peter's got Meghan, he doesn't really care what I'm doing."

Her heart was thudding in her head now, pounding a sensual beat of warning against her brain.

"There has to be a way out," she said quickly. She knew she sounded a little desperate but she didn't care. Desperate times called for freaking out. "Did you try all the keys?"

"The only key that fit is in the lock now," he replied calmly. "It won't open the security bolts, though. I'm assuming they are a part of the theft deterrent system. They probably require a code or special passkey or something."

That made sense. Larissa turned the key anyhow. It twisted. She heard the locks disengage. But the bolts didn't move.

She grabbed the etched brass handles of the door and shook it as hard as she could, ignoring Jason's laugh behind her.

Echoing his earlier move, she rested her forehead against the glass and tried to gather her thoughts.

They were too scattered, though. Hearing footsteps, she turned to see that Jason was halfway down the mall.

"Where are you going?" she called to his retreating back.

"While you bruise your fists on the doors, I'm going to scout things out. See if I can find food, water or maybe an alternate exit that those keys might open." He glanced back and gave her a wink. "Don't scuff those pretty shoes kicking the door, though."

Leave it to him to go into super scout mode while she hyperventilated. And yes, she frowned, she had considered kicking the stupid door. This was exactly the reason she'd hated taking trips with him. He'd always babied them down for her, and she'd still come off as a total incompetent.

She hated that feeling.

"Maybe you'd rather I use them to kick your—"

"Temper, temper," he chided. He stopped at an unmarked, solid door between two glass-fronted stores and gave her a patient look. "You wanna wait here or come with me?"

And there it was, the question that had defined their relationship.

Only this time, Larissa didn't have to think about the choices. She folded the blanket over her arm, stopping at the still open door to her—because dammit, after all of this, it'd damned well better end up hers—store and tossed it in a box. Then, her still unscuffed heels clattering loudly over the marble floor, she hurried to Jason's side.

"What if we crawled through the air vents," she suggested, noticing one high above the doors, halfway toward the vaulted ceiling.

"That'd be a no," Jason told her as he opened the unmarked door for her to enter first.

"Why?" she asked. "You climb mountains and shimmy up trees for coconuts. But you won't crawl through a suburban vent?"

"That vent would only take us to some other part of the hotel. Did you want to move to a room with a bed, perhaps?"

Hell, no.

Larissa hurried through the doorway into the dark hall. She didn't want to be a chicken, but as soon as Jason let go of that door, what little light there was would vanish. Not that she was afraid of the dark, but wandering through a strange place in absolute darkness with Jason felt like a really bad idea to her. Who knew what she might accidentally touch.

"We're going to have trouble finding anything we need without some sort of light," Jason said, echoing the saner part of her thoughts. "Maybe if we prop the door open, we'll be able to see."

Larissa arched a doubtful brow. She could barely make out anything halfway down the hall now.

"I don't suppose you keep a little flashlight in your purse," he mused.

"No." Then remembering, she turned back to face him. "I do have a book of matches I got as a favor from the wedding I attended last weekend, though."

His face was in shadows and the wince was infinitesimal, but she still caught it.

"They're matches, Jason. Not marriage cooties."

He gave a short, rueful laugh and shrugged. "Nothing personal."

"Of course not. As far as I know, I was the closest you ever got to a wife. So, there's no reason for me to take your feelings about it personally."

Impatient, Larissa brushed past Jason, pretending that the feel of his body against hers didn't make her want to close that door and let the dark keep their secrets.

"Where are you going?" he asked.

"To get the cootie matches," she tossed over her shoulder as she stalked away from him.

She was still stomping when she reached her purse, where she'd left it on the counter of her soon-to-be store. She didn't unzip the leather bag yet, though. Instead she draped her arms across the countertop and laid her forehead against the cool marble, trying to chill out.

"Keep your eyes on the prize," she lectured herself. She

used a couple more deep belly-breaths to get her thoughts in order.

Being trapped was definitely high on her sucky list. And being trapped with Jason was even higher, right under flood, famine and worldwide illiteracy. But that wasn't the big picture, it was simply a tiny roadblock. She just had to remember that.

The priority here was that she get the store. Which meant that Jason couldn't get it. So if she was going to be stuck here—with him, anyhow—she might as well find some way of turning it to her advantage.

It was all about having the right attitude. Being bitchy and defensive would get her nowhere. If anything, losing control like that just meant that she was giving Jason that much more power, even if he didn't realize it. And knowing Jason, he probably did, and would use it to keep the upper hand. She already had enough to deal with fighting off her attraction to him.

So just like she'd done earlier, when she'd put a lid on her snarky attitude with Conner's partner, she'd paste on a pleasant smile and put her energy into sealing the deal. She'd either convince Jason that she was more deserving of the store or she'd find enough out about why he wanted it and use that to convince him to go in a different direction.

Easy peasy.

And how pathetic was it to lie to oneself? Rolling her eyes, but back in control, she got the matches from her purse and turned toward the doorway. Her gaze landed on the box of merchandise she'd packed away.

A wide smile curved her lips and she knelt down to unwrap one of the scented candles. See. Chill out and get her head on straight and things were already going her way.

She lit the decadently scented soy wax and headed back to join Jason. She wasn't surprised to see he hadn't waited.

One hand cupped around the flame to keep it safe, she made her way down the hall, pretending she wasn't wigged out by the long, spidery shadows her fingers cast on the walls.

There were three doors at the end of the hall. Jason had propped one open with a chair. She could hear the occasional thump and four-letter word, so she knew he was in there. Pausing in the doorway, she squinted through the dark.

"Score," Jason said, obviously hearing her less than stealthy entrance. "It looks like the construction workers keep some food in here. Roach coach sandwiches, bottled water, a little of this and that."

Larissa's eyes adjusted, so she could make out the dim outline of tables, chairs and counters. The candlelight reflected off the door of the stainless steel refrigerator Jason was looking into. He glanced over his shoulder and gave an approving nod toward the candle.

"Clever. Part of your inventory?"

"Yes. It's the Passionflower by Moonlight scent. Chloe makes them," she told him as she stepped farther into the room. Holding the candle high, she looked around and tried to tell herself that this was the comfy space where she'd be having lunches soon. And not a creepy potential scene from every horror movie that ever started with a blackout.

"Chloe made that candle?" His arms full of what looked like food, Jason let the refrigerator door swing shut. "I thought all she made was trouble. How's she doing now?"

"She's good. Busy with her many businesses, yet still finding time for trouble," Larissa said with a shrug. Jason and Chloe had gotten along really well, kind of like brother and sister with a mutual passion for smart-ass dialogue, movies that blew things up and their love for Larissa herself. Which probably accounted for why Chloe had taken their breakup so personally.

"I'm glad. Both that she's doing good and that she hasn't lost that troublemaker side. Tell her hi for me, okay?"

Tell her that the guy with the magic dick said hi? Chloe would love that. "I'll tell her. I doubt she's going to want to hear it, though."

Jason emptied his armload onto a table next to a pile of stuff Larissa hadn't noticed before. She joined him to see what he'd collected. Some bottles of water, a brick of unopened cheese, sandwiches in plastic, a couple of apples and a large bag of chips. There was also a roll of paper towels.

"At least we won't get hungry," she commented. "Wasn't there a vending machine, though?"

"Yup. But it's digital and it went down with the power. I'll leave some cash and a note to cover this food, though."

"Well, aren't you both responsible and resourceful," she teased.

"Tricks of the trade," he dismissed with a modest shrug. "So why won't Chloe want my greeting? I thought she liked me."

"Sure," Larissa agreed, leaving her candle on the table as she started rooting through cupboards and drawers to see what she could add to his stash. "She liked you when we were a couple."

"She doesn't like me anymore?" He sounded like a pouting little boy who'd just been told Santa wasn't real.

Larissa added a sleeve of saltine crackers and, oh yeah, a handful of chocolate bars to the stash. "Well, let's put it this way. She burned your effigy in a bonfire the Halloween after we split up."

"Ouch."

"You were naked," Larissa told him, only gloating a little. "And you were really, really small. If you know what I mean."

Grimacing, Jason's hand twitched toward the fly of his

jeans. Larissa turned away to hide her smirk. Seeing a box on the floor next to one of the cabinets, she brought it over to carry their booty.

She sighed at the pile of food. They wouldn't really need to eat that, would they? Someone had to come for them soon. Maybe? Hopefully?

Not likely. Her shoulders sagged as she started packing food into the box.

"Was this at her annual Halloween bash? The one that usually has a guest list of, oh, a hundred people?"

"It was closer to one-fifty that year."

He sighed.

"Any anonymity?"

"Well, she labeled the effigy with your name and recited a poem before she tossed it into the flames. So, nope." The box filled, Larissa lifted it, then glanced at the candle on the table. She couldn't carry both. Before she could figure it out, Jason reached around her to take the box from her arms. His hands left heated little tingles of awareness as they brushed hers, his arms practically embracing her from the side. Larissa swallowed, trying to clear the lump from her throat.

She was glad he had a hold of the box since she'd probably have dropped it at his feet otherwise.

"I'm sorry I missed the event," he said in a husky tone she knew had nothing to do with Chloe or effigies. But it had everything to do with fire. Her eyes wandered over his face, all intriguing shadows and angles in the candlelight. God, the man was gorgeous. Even clearly irritated, he still looked good enough to lick from head to toe.

"You can probably catch it on YouTube," she said breathlessly. She watched closely, hoping to see anger on his face. That would go such a long way toward making him less drool-worthy.

Instead he threw back his head and laughed. The sound echoed through the dark room, wrapping around her like a good-natured hug. Damn him. Why couldn't he be a full-time jerk? It'd be so much easier to dislike him.

"I'LL HAVE TO LOOK IT UP," Jason said, trying to control his laughter. He probably should be irritated to be publicly mocked, but as long as Larissa wasn't the one commenting on his…size, he figured it was just good fun. "Leave it to Chloe to find an original and creative insult."

"She's a wonder," Larissa agreed with a smile that said she'd probably bookmarked that YouTube page. She glanced around the break room. "It looked like we've gotten everything useful, doesn't it?"

She lifted the candle and, hand curved to protect the flame, headed toward the door.

"Did you see what the other rooms were already?" she asked.

"Janitor's closet and storage," he said, hefting the box a little higher and following her. "I couldn't see much without light, but from what I could make out, the storage room has a series of lockers, all secured. And unless we want to scrub floors, there wasn't much in the janitor's closet, either. I didn't find any bathrooms, though. That could be an issue."

This was the problem with being trapped in an urban setting instead of a remote island somewhere. Sure, they had shelter and didn't have to climb trees for their coconut dinner. But he didn't think Conner would appreciate it if Jason peed on those pricey plants lining the center of that mall.

"Actually, there's a public restroom in the hall across the mall, but Conner mentioned that it's not outfitted with toilets yet. But there are private bathrooms in each of the stores. I checked and the one in my store isn't locked."

"My store," Jason muttered with a frown. Why was she so sure she'd get the space? He had a much stronger track record and already had a successful business. She had a fluffy romantic dream. And, he had to admit, the nicest ass he'd ever seen.

He wanted to ask if she was dating Conner now, but figured she'd blow up like she had the last time he'd asked that question. But that was probably why she was so confident that she'd edge him out. Because she had the inside track.

Jason's gut burned at the idea of anyone other than him being with Larissa. The idea of her with Conner, a guy who could offer her the world, plus her perfect store space, made the burn flame even higher.

And those guys with Conner had definitely been checking her out. Which meant that even if they tried to spout some crap about professionalism in choosing, they were leaning her way.

Despite their history, Jason didn't want to hurt her and take away her dream. But he needed that store. The future of Can-Do was on the line. Despite his friendship with Daniel, Conner was obviously going to be on Larissa's side. And given that his ass didn't look nearly as good in a skirt, Jason had absolutely no way of influencing the other guys on the committee.

Which left Larissa. Jason eyed the way her jacket ruffled across those curvy hips. His gaze slid down the narrow black skirt covering way too much of her legs, then dropped to those sexy little shoes in do-me red.

They were stuck together for the next little while, so even though she probably wanted to, she couldn't run away. And as long as he kept his eye on the prize—which was scoring that store space—he could dial back his predator instincts and try and be a gentleman long enough to find a way to talk her out of taking such a huge business risk. Diplomacy and circumspection. He could handle that.

At least, he thought he could.

"It sounds like all our needs are covered, then," he said, referring to his concern over a bathroom.

When they reached the store, he dumped the box on the counter. Larissa set the candle down. He watched her cast a look around the store, kind of like those looks moms gave to their funny-looking newborn babies. Love, pride and a blind sort of surety that it was the greatest-looking thing in the world. He squinted a look at the bare walls and modern fixtures and shrugged.

It definitely wasn't his style, that was for sure. But he wouldn't have thought it to be Larissa's, either.

"You really like this space?" he asked. "I mean, I thought you wanted your bookstore to be in one of those fancy old houses. Something with a lot of character and, what was it? Charm?"

"Well, sure, that's what I wanted." She looked both surprised and cautious. "But that was before. Now I know that to make my dream a reality, I have to make certain... adjustments."

"You? Adjust? You're kidding, right?" Jason winced. That hadn't been very diplomatic.

"I can adjust," she protested, crossing her arms across her chest. The lift of her chin and her tone were both defensive. "Unlike some people who refuse to compromise, I'm excellent at adjusting and doing whatever it takes to make something work."

"And I'm not?"

"I didn't say that."

"You implied it."

"No." She shook her head, sending her curls bouncing

over her shoulders. "I said I've adjusted and worked on perfecting my plans for the future. And since you're considering totally changing how you operate your business by trying to shoehorn it into a store, you're obviously willing to adjust."

"From the sound of it, you don't think much of my plan, though."

So much for circumspection. But if there was one thing Jason had always hated, it was being judged. It made him feel like he had to prove something. And since whipping it out and showing off his size wasn't the answer, he'd have to find another way.

He just wasn't sure what, since he had plenty of doubts about this crazy scheme. But he wasn't telling her that. He'd learned early on that life was all about impressions. He kept a confident, assured demeanor, whether he got lost guiding a tour through the Amazon or if he got up in the middle of the night to find the group's campsite surrounded by hyenas. If he acted like he had his shit together, people believed he did. And sooner or later, the act became reality.

"I didn't say what I thought of your ideas, one way or the other," she protested. "I think your business is just that, yours. You've devoted enough of your life to it—you should know what will work or not."

"But you've devoted a lot of your life to learning business." He strode over until he was just inches away. She lifted her chin and glared, but didn't give way. God, he loved it when she got all spunky and brave. "You take classes, read books, made those business plans. Don't you have an opinion on the wisdom of my plans?"

He had no idea why he was doing this. It was some twisted form of masochism. Or maybe he just needed her to say something strong enough to piss him off, since he was having rotten luck convincing himself to keep his hands off of her.

"What difference does it make if I think changing your business is a good idea or not?" she challenged, looking more curious than pissed. "My opinion never mattered to you before."

"Of course it did," he countered. Then he grinned wickedly and gave in to temptation. He reached out to lift one of those soft curls from her shoulder and rubbed the silky length between his fingers.

She stiffened, like she wanted to pull away but didn't want him to know he was getting to her. Good. He wanted her edgy. He wanted her to reach the same level of sexual hyper-awareness that he was at. He stared at her lips, remembering their softness and sweet flavor.

And how long it'd been since he'd had a taste.

"You don't really need my thoughts. I'm sure you can see just as well as I can that this space is much better suited to my store than your jungle adventures."

"Right," Jason said agreeably, like he wasn't irritated. He shifted to the right, trapping her between his body and the counter. "Better suited. Because it's just about appearances, right? And yet, one of us here has spent the last four years dreaming, planning and talking about a perfect dream. The other of us has been living the dream as a work-in-progress. Which one do you think really counts?"

# 6

"IT'S ABOUT MORE THAN appearances," Larissa defended. "Not all businesses can be built on the concept of spending each day playing, you know. Some of us want to make sure everything is just right before we commit our energy, reputation and finances."

She gave him a pointed look just this side of a smirk. "How'd you start your business again? Wasn't it by borrowing money from your mom so you could take a couple of drunken frat boys kayaking?"

"You're just jealous," Jason teased, his body so close to hers she could feel the heat radiating off his chest.

"Aren't you the jealous one?" she challenged, knowing she was stepping into dangerous territory but willing to risk it if it meant he'd back off.

The teasing look on his face faded, replaced by an intensity that made her stomach take a nosedive. She winced, waiting for the explosion. But it didn't come. Instead, right there before her eyes, he seemed to gather control and pull himself together.

He leaned closer to say, "Sweetheart, the only reason for me to be jealous is if you've found some guy who can make you explode in sexual delight the way I did."

He paused, as if waiting for her to fill him in on her incredible sex life. When she just pressed her lips together, he grinned.

"See, no reason to be jealous," he taunted.

That he was right made her furious. Pulse racing, she stared into Jason's blue eyes. His usual cocky amusement was there, yes. But so was desire. Hot and intense, with the promise of all sorts of orgasmic pleasure.

Oh yeah, he wanted her. She shivered a little and forced herself to pretend her nipples weren't aching and that her panties hadn't suddenly become damp. Her fingers trembled with the need to touch him. Just one more time, to slide her fingers over the hard muscles of his chest. To wrap her hands around the thick muscles of his arms. To...

No! She had to stop this. He gave her a sexy look and she instantly turned into a puddle of lust?

Why did he always get to be the one in control? Why did she always fall, panting at his feet? When did her dreams come true, the ones where *he* fell at *her* feet?

What she'd do once he was groveling at her toes depended, of course, on which dream she happened to be entertaining at the time.

There was the power dream, where she left him in a pathetic heap wanting her like crazy while she turned her back and walked away.

And then there was the sexy dream. Where she made him her love slave and he, following her orders, kissed his way up her leg until things got interesting.

"Maybe you should move back a little," she said, squirming and trying to hide her breathlessness. "Without AC, it's getting pretty hot and stuffy in here."

"You think that's the lack of AC, babe?" He shook his head, a few strands of sun-kissed hair falling across his forehead. "What kind of guy are you seeing that you'd confuse horniness with humidity? Has your love life become that boring?"

What love life? The only sexual variety she got these days was in choosing between her D-cell powered friend and the shower massage. Not that Jason needed to know that.

Especially when she was sure his love life was full and varied. Jason was any woman's perfect man. Gorgeous and sexy with a hard body that promised endless hours of plea-surable exploration. A fun, engaging personality that made good on the charm his smile promised. And then there was that dangerous hint of bad boy that any woman with man-radar could tell meant he knew all the naughty tricks, even if he'd only stick around long enough for one round of show-and-tell.

"I'm sure it's the lack of AC. Either that, or your ego has become its own heat source," she snapped, blinking away the sting of tears. Frustration, she told herself. It had to be that and not some insane form of jealousy. She tried to move around him, but he sidestepped to block her escape.

"My ego does provide a lot of heat," he agreed. "But it's fueled by plenty of references."

Larissa rolled her eyes. That was enough. Needing some breathing room, she pressed her hands to his chest to push him away. He didn't budge.

He did make a little growly sound of appreciation in the back of his throat though.

She yanked her hands back.

"You'd better watch yourself," he teased, as if he could read her thoughts. "We're not only fighting the lure of can-dlelight but we've got super-koteka there, giving off all that sexual mojo."

"Right, with all that temptation, there's no way I'll be able to control myself," she replied, her mouth getting ahead of her brain again. "Because you're such a stud and all."

She immediately wanted to grab the words back. Not because she was a verbal wimp. Nope, she wanted them back because she was another kind of wimp. The look on Jason's face, intense, focused and a little pissed, sent warning sirens off in her mind. That look reminded her, in no uncertain terms, that she was a complete sexual wimp. The kind who couldn't say no to temptation.

That was his "dare me" look. The look that he got when he went off to climb death-defying mountains. When he'd jumped out of a perfectly good airplane. When he wanted to make love.

Eek, she silently squeaked.

"I don't suppose you're considering skydiving," she asked desperately.

"Not even close," he said, stepping closer. Close enough that the heat from his body was probably steaming away any wrinkles in her silk jacket.

"Mountain climbing? A trip down a crocodile-infested river in a canoe?"

"I had something a little more exciting in mind," he confessed, his words husky as took her hand and lifted it to his mouth.

Her knees nearly buckled. Of course he had something else in mind.

"Rappelling in the Painted Desert?" she suggested softly, remembering the time he'd convinced her that dropping herself off the side of a mountain would be fun. He'd used sex in that argument, too.

His grin told her that his memories of that trip were just as hot as hers. Larissa's stomach gave a slow, twisty dive. She pressed her thighs together to stop the trembling, but the movement only added to the wet need pulsating between her legs.

"You know what I remember?" he asked quietly.

How her screams of ecstasy had echoed through the canyon the night they'd camped at the base of the mountain?

"What?" she whispered, her eyes glued to his lips. Her fingers ached with the need to touch him. To run her hands over his chest and feel the heat of his bare skin beneath her palms.

"I remember that you babble when you're nervous." He shifted, angling his body lower, so his face was level with hers. "So what's up, Larissa? You nervous about something?"

"Uncomfortable isn't the same as nervous," she said, sidestepping the issue. Because even though they both knew damned well she was nervous, she wasn't about to admit it.

"What's to be uncomfortable about?"

The distinct possibility of exploding from sexual overload. Probably better to keep that to herself, though.

"You're kidding, right? We're trapped inside an unfinished mall with borrowed food, no air conditioning and no way to tell anyone in the outside world we're here," she growled, frustration rising with each word until she hit a dog-calling pitch. Just in case that wasn't enough, she threw her arms in the air to emphasize her aggravation. "I'm trying to launch a new career and finally find the perfect venue that fits my dream to a tee. And what happens? You show up. You. Of all freaking people."

"Were there other freaking people you'd rather be trapped with?" he asked, taking both of her hands in his. Probably to keep their irritated punctuations from poking him in the eye.

"I'd rather not be trapped at all." She tried to tug her hands away. He didn't let go.

"Well, we are, so we might as well take advantage of the situation, right?"

Wrong. Wrong, wrong, wrong. Shaking her head, Larissa tried to find the words to protest. But his fingers were rubbing over hers in soft, gentle swirls that made her insides go gooey. He lifted her fingers to his mouth and brushed a warm kiss over her knuckles. She almost whimpered as he stared over her hands, his eyes filled with wicked temptation.

"You never answered my question," Jason said, his words husky and low.

"What question?"

"Are you single?" He pressed her hands to his chest, then curved his along her waist.

"Does it matter?"

"Yeah," he said, his mouth coming closer and closer. "Yeah, it does matter."

"Why?" she breathed, her words a whisper against his lips.

"Because you're going to feel really bad making time with me if there is some poor schmuck waiting at home for you," he said just before his mouth took hers.

She wanted to protest. In a heartbeat, her mind was ready to pitch an entire argument about assumptions and cockiness. But, as always when it came to Jason, her body overruled her brain.

Besides, given that just the soft press of his lips to hers had her melting, she was pretty sure his cocky assumption was right. The man had always had a special way with the cock.

His mouth teased. His lips were soft, gently rubbing over hers then slipping away. Tiny little kisses that had her panting. Wanting, needing, more.

She clutched his arms, her fingers clinging to his rock-hard biceps. Passion she hadn't felt in years exploded, swirling through her body. Her nipples ached, pressing through the layers of fabric as if pleading for his attention. The tight, hot bud of desire pulsed between her thighs, begging for release. She shifted her hips, trying to press herself to the hard length of his thigh. She tried to slide her right foot along the strong muscles of his calf, but couldn't lift it more than a half-foot.

She bit back a frustrated groan. Useless. The tight A-line of her skirt was as good as a chastity belt, keeping her thighs locked together. She didn't know whether to cry or celebrate. The skirt was probably the only thing keeping her from rubbing against him like a cat in heat.

But knowing she couldn't take her pleasure gave her a freedom she wouldn't have allowed otherwise. Using it like a safety net, she gave herself permission to have as much fun as possible with her thighs closed.

Still pressed against his chest where he'd left them, her fingers relaxed. For just a second she reveled in the feel of his heart beating beneath her palms. She smoothed her hands over the hard planes of his chest, the soft cotton of his shirt a delicious contrast. Needing to see if the body she'd reveled in memorizing still felt the same, she slipped her hands up to his shoulders, then down the hard, rounded muscles of his biceps. She moaned in the back of her throat.

His body was a work of art. A tool he'd honed to perfection on his long treks up mountains, over waterfalls and into jungles. A tool, she remembered, that he wielded with precision when it came to lovemaking.

Their kiss intensified. She sipped at the rich taste of him, sucking his tongue deeper into her mouth. His moan filled her with sensual power.

Romance was her priority. It was her life.

But right now, in this moment, she'd be happy with sex. Because Jason's tool was the best she'd ever had. And she'd love to use it, just one more time.

OH, GOD, SHE TASTED GOOD. Like strawberries and cream, drizzled in chocolate with just a hint of something alcoholic that would knock him on his ass before he realized it.

Jason's entire being was in conflict. His body was loving the feel of Larissa's sweet little curves pressed against him again. His brain was doing that mocking head shake, clearly not impressed with his inability to stick with the plan. He was just supposed to intimidate her a little, then convince her to back off of this store idea. And some other part of him, he'd call it his heart because his soul sounded so drippy, that part gave a big ole sigh of relief, as if it'd just come home after a long, lonely trek.

Like he did anything that threatened to get in the way of his pleasure, Jason ignored it.

Kissing Larissa was much more important. He slipped his hands through the tangled jungle of her curls, loving the silky way her hair grabbed at his fingers. Like she was holding onto him, willing him to get closer. His mouth slanted, taking their kiss deeper. Tongues danced, smooth and sleek, against each other. Shifting his fingers, he pressed them against the back of her head, pulling her tighter against his body.

Her breasts brushed against his chest softly. His dick hardened like steel, the length of it throbbing painfully against his zipper.

He told himself to behave. A kiss. He was only giving in to the desire to kiss her. Just one taste, after such a long time of going without.

Then she gave a soft, purring kind of moan and pressed a little harder, her breasts flattening against his beating heart.

Screw behaving.

He slipped one hand from her hair and brushed his fingers gently down the length of her neck. He skimmed the soft ruffled fabric of her collar until he reached the top button that held the jacket closed.

Her breath caught, the action pressing the lush curve of her breast against his fingers. Jason felt the hesitation in her kiss. Before she had time to solidify her doubt and tell him to stop, he brushed his fingers over the tip of her breast. Her nipple pebbled against the back of his fingers. In gentle, barely touching her sweeps, he brushed his knuckles across the peak once. Twice, then again a third time.

She groaned, nipping at his lower lip in a sharp little bite that sent a shaft of desire all the way to the tip of his dick. Without thinking, Jason pulled his other hand from her hair and slid it down to cup her ass, lifting her tight against his painfully hard length.

One-handed, he made quick work of the tiny, fabric covered buttons of her jacket until he reached the last one at her waist. He pushed the fabric off one shoulder and pulled his mouth from hers. Her protest was a high-pitched moan.

He buried his face in the curve of her neck to breathe in her scent—soft floral and a sweetness that was all Larissa. His fingers traced the lacy edge of her camisole, knowing she'd worn the sexy little piece of lingerie for herself since that jacket thing modestly covered all the good stuff.

He had to see. Had to know if she looked as good as he remembered.

Jason pulled back a little, taking in the sight with hooded eyes. Lush breasts, surprising given her tiny body, spilled over a frothy concoction of satin and lace. He couldn't tell the exact color in the candlelight, something between a red and a pink. Like raspberries.

He swallowed.

Damned if she didn't look even better than he remembered.

"I love that you wear this kind of thing," he whispered,

giving in to the need to press damp, open-mouthed kisses along her throat.

Her head fell back to give him greater access as she murmured, "What kind of thing? Underwear?"

"Underwear is plain and cotton. Kind of like vanilla. Useful but not really exciting," he decided, his teeth snagging one tiny satin strap and tugging it aside so her shoulder was bare. That pulled the pale fabric of the camisole tighter against her breasts, drawing it taut over the pouty points. He swallowed hard.

"There's nothing vanilla about you, or the sexy little things you wear."

Their height difference a challenge he'd solved years back, he looked around quickly, then wrapped his hands around her waist and effortlessly lifted. Her hands gripped his shoulders for balance as he set her on the counter.

"Jason—"

He could see the sexual fog clearing from her eyes, concern and way too much sanity starting to shine in those dark depths.

Nope, definitely not the look he wanted.

Quickly, he kissed her again. A swipe of his tongue over her lips was all it took to get her to open that delicious mouth to him. Her lips were warm and inviting, even though her hands on his shoulders pressed against him like she was making sure he didn't get any closer.

A challenge?

Perfect.

He stepped up his game, taking the kiss deeper as he slipped his tongue in, out, then in again to mimic the slow, heady pleasure he'd have sliding the hard length of his dick into the welcoming warmth of her body.

His hand swept down her smooth arm to her elbow, then slid back up to curve down the side of her torso. Her breath caught. He could feel her anticipation build as the side of his hand brushed against the heavy weight of her breast.

Her gasping little moan sent a shaft of desire straight through his body. Muscles taut, he reminded himself not to get carried away. This was just a little fun. A little kiss for old times' sake. He was in control here.

He moved his hand slowly, oh-so-slowly, back up the same path along her torso. But this time, his palm cupped her breast. Barely touching, just a hint of pressure, as if he was sensing the delicious weight rather than holding it.

Her fingernails dug into his biceps.

Screw control.

He shifted, taking her breast into his hand. The hardened tip nudged his palm. He curved his fingers under the lace of her silky little top so he was gripping it. It took all his restraint not to give it one swift rip so he could get to the barely hidden treasure. But destroying Larissa's underwear would probably ruin the mood. At least, for her.

Instead he dipped deeper, rubbing the backs of his knuckles over the hard bud. It felt like pebbled velvet. He wanted—needed—to see more.

He slowly, reluctantly, pulled his mouth from hers. He hated to leave that delicious pleasure, but his need was too high. He took a second to take in her face, all sharp angles and those huge, huge eyes staring back languidly. Then he dropped his gaze to her candlelit chest.

Her skin was so pale, even in the flickering light, he could see the faint pattern of veins as her heart beat a rapid tattoo right above her silky top.

His body tense, his nerve endings all zinging in anticipation, he slowly used one finger to slide a strap down her arm. The top dropped a little. He held his breath, but the lace caught on her beaded nipple. He could see the rosy point through the delicate threads like a ripe raspberry hidden by frothy sugar. A deliciously teasing temptation.

Concentration narrowing to a pinpoint, he rubbed the tip of his forefinger over the lace. Her nipple puckered even tighter. Her breath shuddered, making her breast bounce gently against his skin.

Slowly, all of his moves careful and deliberate, he settled her knees to one side of his thighs. Then he leaned closer so Larissa had to tilt backward, her hands propping her up in a half sitting, half lying position.

"I dream of you," he confessed beneath his breath just before taking that plump tip into his mouth. His tongue swirled as he gently sucked on her flesh. She tasted so good. The lace added an extra layer of surreal delight to the experience. Between the candlelight and the lack of any sound other than Larissa's gentle moans, it was like he was in a dream.

A very tasty, very erotic, very tempting dream that made him wish for things he'd long since given up as impossible.

Like sweet Larissa.

Bittersweet pain layered over the fervent delight pounding through his body as he remembered that, as good as she tasted, as much as he wanted her, this road was a dead end. Larissa was a forever girl and he was all about the present moment.

He rasped his tongue over her burgeoning flesh. His muscles tensed at Larissa's gasp. She was so responsive, her body so tuned in to his own desires, it was like his wildest dream was coming true right before his eyes. And right under his tongue.

So if the present moment was all he could get, he'd wring every drop of pleasure from it he could.

Focused on that, he pushed the lace away with his tongue

while his other hand slid the opposite strap down her arm. The fabric dropped, framing her breasts in a silken cradle for his enjoyment.

His fingers traced a delicate pattern over one breast, sliding over the tip so she gasped, then cupping and holding the weight up for his kisses. Gently at first, he brushed his lips over one tip, then the other. His kisses got hotter. His teeth nipped, his fingers plucked the delicate flesh into tighter pebbles of delight.

More, his body shouted.

He slid his tongue up her slender throat, then took her mouth in a voracious, hot and wet kiss. Teeth, tongue and lips slid together in a wild dance. Knowing he was pushing his luck, hoping she was turned on enough to let him, he slipped one hand along her side until he found the button and zipper holding her straight jacket masquerading as a skirt closed. A flick of his fingers and he loosed the fabric.

His mouth still on hers, he used his torso to press her backward so she lay lengthwise down the counter. Her hands roamed his shoulders before she slid one inside the open collar of his shirt. Her fingernails scraped a trail of ecstasy along his chest and she gave a low purr that vibrated through his body like thunder.

With open-mouthed kisses, he made his way down to her chest. Unable to help himself, he stopped to pay special homage with a flick of his tongue to each straining nipple before kissing his way down the curve of her breasts to her stomach. He nibbled at the soft flesh, his hands going to the loosened waistband of her skirt. As if she'd just realized what he'd done, her body tensed. He pulled one hand from the skirt, sliding his palm in the opposite direction of his mouth until he cupped her breast, his fingers creating a sensual distraction.

It was only when he felt her relax again, her muscles

softening, her focus on the pleasure he was giving her instead of worrying about what he was up to, that he pressed his kisses lower. He nudged the skirt down to bare her belly, kissing the sweet indention before swirling his tongue in, then out. A little shudder rocked through her body, sending a shaft of pleasure through him.

He kissed lower, taking the skirt down as he went. When the fabric caught at her hips, he winced, knowing his sneaky plan of descent was in jeopardy. Larissa shifted. He moved fast, sliding her skirt off her legs in a single swift tug. Before it hit the floor he had his fingers inside her panties.

Knowing she could call it quits at any time, he went right for the gusto. Draping her knees over his shoulders, he spread her legs wide.

She gave a high, keening cry of pleasure when he rubbed his thumb along her swollen clit and he knew he had her. Tension poured from his shoulders and he let himself relax and give over to the moment.

A tiny scrap of lace masqueraded as her panties. He didn't waste time pulling them off her hips. It was faster, easier, to slide it aside so he could have full access to her wet delight.

His fingers slid into her tight sheath, swirling and dancing to the rhythm of her hips as she rose to meet his thrusting digits. He breathed in her musky scent and groaned, then licked her like an ice cream cone.

Already primed, she went off like a rocket. A cry of shocked pleasure ripped through her. She grabbed his shoulders, whether for traction as she raised her hips or to make sure he didn't stop, he didn't know. Didn't care.

He sucked the dewy fold between his teeth.

"Oh, God," she gasped hoarsely.

He nipped, then soothed her with his tongue. Her *Oh, God* became a chanting entreaty.

His fingers found her rhythm. His tongue matched it. Knowing she was right there on the edge, he reached up to give her nipple a little tug.

She exploded. Her chants became a keening cry of ecstasy. Her body tensed, as if she were holding on to the orgasm as tight as she could. Then she surrendered, her hips falling back to the counter and her entire body relaxed.

Shudders, tiny little tremors, quaked through her body. The sound of her labored gasps echoed through the room, music to his ears. The sharp bite of her fingernails in his shoulders eased. Consciously or not, she rubbed the tips of her fingers over the flesh she'd just gripped so tightly as if trying to ease the sting.

He wanted her like crazy. He needed the feel of her hot, tight body sheathing his. Milking the pleasure from him until he was spent. His dick throbbed painfully, begging for release.

Jason dropped his head against her belly, his face pressed to the smooth warmth. He knew what was in his wallet down to the exact dollar, the placement of every credit card because he'd watched customs dig through it just that morning.

And nowhere in there, or anywhere else on his person, was anything resembling a condom. He wanted to scream in frustration.

He licked his lips and lifted his head, smiling at the sight of her, all mussed and heavy eyed. Color warmed her to a soft rosy shade, from her cheeks to her tasty nipples.

Regret twined with frustration at the sight. In that second, he wished everything could be different. That he could be different. He wanted to promise her anything if it'd give them another chance.

But he'd done that once already. And the results had pretty much sucked.

So all he said was, "Yum."

# 7

YUM?

Her head spinning, Larissa didn't know if she was supposed to thank him for the climax, or, well, thank him for stopping.

Her body was still shaking with pleasure, orgasmic aftertremors shuddering through her as Jason pressed another kiss to her hypersensitive belly before pulling away from her.

He gave a pained wince as he straightened. Her gaze automatically dropped to his crotch, where his erection was looking like The Incredible Hulk, ready to rip itself free of his jeans.

She licked her lips. Oh, yeah. Yum, indeed.

He pulled away, his back cracking through the room like a slap, pulling her out of her sexual fog.

Of course his body was protesting. He was sporting a redwood-sized hard-on.

Before, she'd have played *this for that*. Because the man was so freaking amazing at this, she loved giving him that.

But this wasn't before. And the only thing they'd ever

had that was real between them was sex. A fact she needed to remember.

Suddenly very aware of how naked she was, in more ways than one, Larissa sat upright, pulling her camisole straps back over her shoulders and adjusting her panties. Avoiding his eyes, she slipped her legs to the edge of the counter, but before she could hop down, Jason reached out. His hands wrapped around her waist, so big and warm, and he lifted her gently to her feet.

Tears stung her eyes. Why did he have to be so damned sweet? Couldn't he just be incredible in bed? Just be good at the sex stuff and useless at melting her heart? She wanted to punch him in the arm, he made her so angry. He was everything she wanted in a man. But he was everything she didn't want, too.

"That was a mistake," she muttered, looking around for her skirt and jacket, hoping they'd offer some modesty. Her jacket was there hanging on the edge of the counter. She snagged it and shoved her arms into the sleeves so hard she was surprised she didn't rip the delicate fabric.

"Am I supposed to apologize?" Jason asked with a laugh that stopped somewhere between pain and irritation. "You weren't shoving my head away, babe. So I figured you were having yourself a pretty good time. If I had a condom, I'm betting we'd be making each other see stars right about now."

Just as angry with herself as she was with him, Larissa shrugged. After a quick glare at the useless chastity belt of a skirt, she scooped it up. It only took a second to decide that wiggling into it would only make the situation worse, so she snagged the soft blanket that had started all this trouble and wrapped it around herself.

"What are you doing?"

"I'm going to get dressed," she said, clutching her skirt

in her fist and heading to the bathroom at the back of the store. Realizing she'd be dressing in a strange pitch black room, she hesitated.

Jason heaved a loud sigh and, walking so stiffly she winced with guilt, he scooped another candle from box and handed it to her. "I don't have the cootie matches so you're on your own for getting it lit."

Larissa pulled her gaze from the long, hard length pressing in painful relief against his zipper before she did something crazy, like drop the blanket. But darn it, she'd been raised with the concept of one good turn deserves another, and if she'd ever seen something worth turning, it was straining that zipper.

No. Their little sexual reunion had been a mistake. A wonderful, mind blowing, deliciously wonderful mistake. Compounding one mistake with another would be crazy. Feel and taste great, but still… "No!"

"Huh?"

"Nothing." She grimaced, then gave him an apologetic look and took the candle. Not willing to bend over and dig through the box, given the naked state of her butt, even covered with a fluffy blanket, she tilted the other candle until the fresh wick took flame.

Sex, even great sex, wasn't worth giving up her romantic values for. She'd tried that once—with Jason himself, as a matter of fact—and it'd bitten her in the ass. No, romance was something that would last. It was a give and take, a careful consideration of the other person's needs and a desire to do special little things to make them feel good. Romance was about the little things that said you wanted to build a beautiful future together.

And while she might stretch that definition by pretending she was being considerate in wanting to take care of his needs and desires, there was nothing little about his thing.

She and Jason? Sure he had his romantic moments, like when he'd helped her down from the counter. He had it in him to be sweet and thoughtful. He was a gentleman without making a big deal of it.

But she'd tried to convince herself once that those moments made for a romantic relationship. And usually then, like now, she was doing the convincing while her body was still rocking the wild afterglow of an orgasm.

The reality was, they had no future beyond this power outage.

Pretending that didn't bother her, Larissa took her candle and skirt and hurried her blanket-covered butt to the back room. Once there, she sucked in a deep breath to try and control the tears that'd suddenly flooded her eyes.

She was being silly. It was just emotional overload brought on by the best orgasm she'd had in two years. Nothing to cry about. Well, other than the fact that this just proved that all her orgasms over the last almost-two years had been pretty pathetic.

She put the candle on the bathroom counter, taking care that it was safe. Setting the place on fire was probably a bad idea, given that she had no clue if the alarms became inactive without power.

A quick shake told her the wrinkles were now a permanent feature of her skirt. No matter, it wasn't like she'd ever wear it again anyway.

She stepped into the skirt and with a wiggle of her hips, slid it into place. She avoided looking in the mirror, knowing her candlelit face would tell her way more than she was willing to handle.

Instead, she gathered the blanket and candle again, and

with a deep breath and quick lecture, rejoined Jason in the store.

Except... She looked around. He wasn't there.

"Jason?"

Fear tickled her spine. Visions of horror movies filled her head. It was always the idiot girl who had irresponsible sex that got whacked by the ax-wielding maniac. But was it really irresponsible? They hadn't had actual intercourse, after all. The only potential danger was to her heart, not her health.

Right. Larissa rolled her eyes. She'd try that argument out on the ax-wielder and let him provide a moral compass.

"Jason," she yelled, tossing the blanket on the settee and hurrying to the front of the store.

No response.

Nerves screaming, she looked around for a weapon. Nothing. Then she spied the long, dusty box Jason had tossed on the bench outside the store. Hurrying over, she flipped the lid open and with a grimace, grabbed the three-foot long wooden dick.

It was smooth and weirdly warm beneath her fingers. And heavier than she'd have guessed. Guys hung this from their dicks? Talk about a workout.

Pretending it was just a stick, not an ode to the fragility of the male ego, she hefted it over one shoulder and lifted the candle high in her other hand.

Swallowing hard, she forced herself to walk down the hallway toward the hotel.

"Jason," she called again tentatively.

Her voice sounded like a mouse's squeak. Pathetic.

"Jason?" she yelled this time.

Was that a sound? She stopped so she could hear without the sound of her high heels tapping against the floor to distract her.

Larissa put the candle down on one of the center display counters so she could get a better grip on the dick in case she needed it as a weapon. For the first time, she was glad it was a big dick.

Swallowing the balled up terror stuck in her throat, she took a deep breath and turned the corner.

"That works better with a body in it."

Larissa jumped, screaming. Spinning around, she wielded the wooden dick like a baseball bat, ready to smack the head off the ax-wielder.

Lightning fast, the man jumped backward just before it cracked him in the face. Jason's laughter roared, echoing and bouncing mockingly off the high ceilings.

She could barely make out his features in the dark, which meant he couldn't see her glare, either. But she still offered her death-stare as he bent at the waist, his fists on his thighs because he was howling like a baboon.

"Don't choke on your hilarity," she muttered.

"I'm sorry. But what'd you think you were going to do? Beat me with a hollow stick because I got under your skirt?"

Deciding that sounded more reasonable than the ax-murderer theory, she just shrugged.

"Where'd you go?" she asked, still out of breath as she pressed her hand against her chest to keep her heart from exploding.

Still grinning like a naughty little boy, he pointed at the hotel's entrance to the mall. "I remembered seeing phones by the elevators when we came through. I wanted to see if they worked."

Larissa's chin shot up. The first thing he thought of after sexing her up was an escape route? Wasn't that so freaking typical.

"And?" she asked coolly. It didn't matter. It wasn't like she was hoping he'd stay around or anything.

She suddenly realized she was still clutching the dick, her fingers gripping it so tight that if it'd been a man, it would have twisted clean off. She tossed it to Jason, who easily caught it. To his credit, he didn't say a word, either.

"And they are on a closed-circuit system, only connecting within the hotel itself," he said with a shrug. "I double checked all the doors on that end. Nada. We're still stuck."

"This must be your worst nightmare. Stuck in one place, unable to run off and play when you get bored."

"What's that supposed to mean?"

She remembered his disgust the time she'd confessed that she thought all his trips were his way of escaping the responsibility of their relationship. It'd been their last argument before their breakup. Well, the last one before he'd accused her of cheating on him, of course.

But even then, he hadn't sounded this angry.

Nibbling on her bottom lip, she stared. His face was a study of shadows, giving him an intimidating look she'd never associated with Jason. Before, he'd always been a sexy, fun, sanity-threatening charmer. Someone dangerous to her heart, but otherwise completely safe.

But now? Her heart was still pounding but not from any ax fears. Looming over her, his shoulders twice the width of hers, he looked like he'd be able to kick any ax-murder's butt.

And wasn't that a turn on. Heart still beating way too fast, she turned away to retrieve her candle.

"Larissa?"

"I'm hungry," she said, ignoring his question. He gave her a long look, then shrugged. It was his way of letting her know he saw the game but was willing to let her play.

He fell into step beside her as she hurried back to the store.

"I just ate, but I could go for seconds." Between his mild expression and even tone, it took her a few beats to get the innuendo.

"Cute," she dismissed as if the idea of his tongue between her legs again didn't make her clitoris quiver. She hurried over to the box of food.

She pulled out a couple of sandwiches, a sleeve of cookies and some fruit. With a quick scan, she decided to eat at the bench outside the store instead of at the counter. No point giving Jason any more fuel to tease her over.

"I forgot how hungry you got after sex," he mused, leaning against the arched doorway watching.

"We didn't have sex," she corrected meticulously.

"It tasted like sex to me."

What was she supposed to say to that? Denying it was churlish. Or was it? This was why she wrote rules for romance. Not for sex. Romance was easier to figure out.

She decided that ignoring any references to sex was the only way to handle this situation. At least, it was if she didn't want to end up in that same position again—on her back, legs wrapped around his shoulders.

And she was doing her best to pretend that's not exactly what she wanted.

"ARE YOU HUNGRY? Did you want a sandwich or some fruit?" Larissa asked, giving him a wide berth as she headed out of the store toward the center of the mall. He watched her hips swing temptingly in that damned skirt again, and sighed. She was clearly unwilling to discuss what he'd already eaten. Since he had no clue what to say, either, he let it go.

They'd just go back to pretending all this sexual tension zinging through the hot, heavy air was brought on by the storm outside. One thing you could always count on with Larissa, she was good at keeping those little fantasies alive.

He watched her choose a leather bench situated in the center of the mall, huge frothy green plants flanking her on either side. With the growing humidity and greenery, it was starting to feel like lunch in the tropics. Larissa set the candle on the center of the bench, then placed food around it like a candlelit picnic.

"Jason?" she asked with a frown, reminding him of her invitation to eat. He glanced at his watch. Seven-thirty. Only a couple hours since the power had blown, but long enough that he was pretty sure they were stuck for the night. Might as well fuel up.

"Sure, thanks." Unsure of his next move, or even his next thought, he slowly straightened from the doorway and sauntered over. He took a few seconds to wrap the koteka in its cotton cloth again before shutting it away in its box. Then he slid the box beneath the bench and sat across from her, the food a safe barrier between them.

"So tell me what you've been up to," he said after a couple bites of mediocre ham and swiss on rye. It needed mustard. He'd eaten tree-bark stew and beetles in his time, so the fact that this sandwich basically sucked was ignorable. But ignoring was easier with a distraction. "I thought you'd have your bookstore long before now. What's the deal?"

She gave him a long look. He could almost see the mental debate going on behind those pretty brown eyes. Did she take him up on the safe, innocuous conversation topic? Or did she risk ignoring it, knowing he'd bring the discussion back to something more dangerous, like how much better she'd tasted than this sandwich.

For a few seconds, he wasn't sure if she was going to

answer or not. Finally she gave a little shrug and set the sandwich down in exchange for an apple.

"I realized that I'd be able to build a more successful store, have a better chance at success, if I laid a stronger foundation. So I took some classes, worked on a few sidelines that will enhance the reputation of the store and bring in more customers."

He shook his head, both impressed by how smart she was at business stuff and baffled that she could wait so long to go for something she wanted.

"You already have a degree in English. So what kind of classes did you need?" he asked.

Her mouth full of apple, she gave herself time to finish chewing before explaining, "Marketing, business and some computer courses."

All that to sell a few books? His confusion must have shown on his face because she leaned forward to explain.

"Bookstores are an endangered species these days. I knew I had to change with the market, and to do that I needed a stronger skill set and a better handle on marketing. The business classes just made sense. After all, I'll be running my own and it pays to know how to do it correctly from the get-go."

"Can-Do is doing great, and I never had to take a bunch of classes," he said, his spine stiffening. He didn't know why Larissa's intellectual approach always made him feel defensive. Maybe because he tended to fly by the seat of his pants instead of obsessing beforehand. Which usually worked out just fine.

Except when it didn't, and his business was in jeopardy.

Like now.

He snapped off a bite of his sandwich, grinding it between his teeth.

"Can-Do is a specialty business that's been built on your charm and reputation," Larissa said, her tone dismissive as if she hadn't just given him a huge compliment. "You honed in on a niche market and made it your own. Between your reputation and your connections, you're obviously going to succeed."

Jason frowned, wondering if she actually thought he was a success and not just a lucky asshole.

"Unless, of course, you do something crazy and ruin it," she added, taking another bite of her apple.

Tossing the tasteless sandwich aside, Jason leaned back on the bench and folded his arms over his chest.

"What's that supposed to mean?"

"Huh?" She'd tucked the apple core on a napkin and was now wiping her fingers with another. "What? Oh, you mean ruining the business?"

"Right. What makes you think I'm ruining my business?"

Larissa rolled her eyes. "I didn't say you were. I said you were a success and would stay that way."

"Unless I ruined it," he ground out.

"Feeling a little defensive?" she guessed, poking at her sandwich again before taking a tiny bite.

He gave her a long stare.

"All I meant was that even successes can fail if they aren't careful. You've built a consistent message with Can-Do. Adventures with a smile. Fun trips, affordable deals, appealing locales."

She waited for him to nod, which he finally did with a short jerk of his chin. He felt like she was luring him into a corner, waiting to spring the trapped door open so he landed on his ass.

"You've got a solid brand. You always were good about keeping your customer database current, so I'm sure you have a list you can tap anytime to tempt them with some special trip or other."

He shrugged one shoulder. "Yeah. That's all SOP. Actually, you're the one who setup our database way back when," he reminded her. "We've added a few search options. We can pull up preferences, like time of year, continents and even travel style. It is pretty solid."

"See," she said. "You've got it handled."

He'd feel a lot better if she'd met his eyes when she'd said that.

"But?"

"But, what?"

"But you think I'm screwing something up. You're tap dancing around it, but I can tell. So spill, what's the problem?"

Larissa avoided his eyes, instead making a show of rewrapping her barely eaten sandwich. She tore open the sleeve of cookies and chose one with delicate precision.

Jason wanted to grab the cookie and send it skittering across the floor, but he knew it wouldn't make her talk any faster. Larissa was gathering her thoughts, marshalling her arguments and adjusting her presentation.

Why couldn't she just blurt it out, tell him what she thought the problem was? It wasn't like he was unreasonable. He'd hear her out. He welcomed insight and constructive criticism, dammit.

Not that there was anything wrong with his plans. He knew his business best. But it would be entertaining to hear whatever crazy problem she'd dreamed up.

If she ever got around to telling him. He bounced his fist off his thigh impatiently. The girl spent more time in her head than she did in real life.

She drove him nuts.

He watched her nibble her way around the circumference

of the cookie. Her teeth took tiny little bites of the crisp chocolate studded wafer. Her pink tongue glistened as she licked a crumb off her lip. He swallowed hard. His dick stirred resentfully, since it was still suffering from painfully unrequited sexual frustration.

Oh yeah, she drove him totally frigging nuts.

"Well, I've already said that I think you've created a solid business," she finally said.

Jason's fist bounced harder.

"And I haven't been following your business the last few years or anything, but from what I know, you're one of the best at what you do. So if you had to make adjustments, you could. Unquestionably."

She took another tiny bite of that cookie. A piece broke away, dropping into the deep vee of her partially rebuttoned jacket. He imagined licking that crumb off her cleavage and felt a light sweat break out on his forehead.

"Adjustments? Why would I have to adjust anything?"

Besides the erection pressing painfully against his belly. A slight shift to the left would ease the pressure, but groping himself seemed a little inappropriate.

"Well…"

"Well, what?"

She wrinkled her nose, grabbing another cookie from the sleeve. She bit it in half with a snap.

"Well, you're obviously already making adjustments, aren't you? You're looking at shifting from depending on your reputation and word-of-mouth to setting up shop in a hotel mall." She glanced down to brush crumbs from her lap and noticed the bit of cookie nestled in her cleavage. With one finger, she scooped it out. It was all he could do not to grab her wrist and carry that delicious crumb to his own mouth.

She glanced back up and caught the look on his face.

Even in the dim light, he could see her fingers tremble as she tossed the crumb onto the napkin along with her apple core.

"So if you're already adjusting, you must have a reason, right?"

He could barely hear her over the rush of lust buzzing around his head. Heads. Then her words filtered through the hunger and he blinked.

"Sure. I wouldn't do it without a good reason."

"And?" This time she was the one doing the prompting.

"And I told you. Peter is settling down. He's cutting his trips down to a dozen or so a year."

"So why change things? Your trips pay for your expenses, right? So you're financially secure. And if Peter's not traveling with Can-Do, won't he get another job?"

"Sure. He's already got a job lined up." He ignored the part about financial security.

"So why tie yourself to a storefront? That kind of long-term anchor seems at odds with the business you've built." Her words were neutral. But her eyes shone with a fervid curiosity.

He couldn't blame her. After all, his refusal to change was one of the core reasons they'd split up. That, and her dating another man. Jason had sometimes wondered if she'd gone out with Conner to push his buttons and force him to choose between her and his traveling.

Jason just stared, his face impassive as he debated answering. It wasn't like his financial responsibilities were a secret, but she didn't know how bad the situation with his mom had become over the last few years. And he didn't like to talk about it. Or to admit, even in a roundabout way, that there was something dragging on his dreams and calling the shots from behind the scenes. It did major damage to his self-image of a free and easy kind of guy.

That, and thinking about it usually made him want to beat the hell out of something.

# 8

LARISSA'S BODY WAS SO TENSE, she felt like she was going to have bruises. She didn't know what was going on in Jason's head, but he looked furious.

She shouldn't have talked to him about business.

Her stomach cramped and tension danced in little black dots in front of her eyes.

They were locked in here for who knew how long and now he was pissed. A tiny trickle of sweat slid down her back. The room, so cool when they'd come in, was starting to take on the damp heat typical of a South Carolina evening storm. And now she could add an angry ex-lover to the mix, just for a little extra discomfort.

She wished they could go back to before, when it'd only been shock and sexual tension filling the air between them.

She should have kept her mouth shut. She knew better. Larissa's romance rule number five: Men are like glaciers—frozen solid and slow to change. Trying to resculpt one was a lesson in frustration, so why bother?

She'd learned that the hard way when she'd thought he'd actually be able to commit to a relationship between them.

Instead, he'd found the first excuse to bail, running back to his freedom as fast as he could.

It wasn't until she saw the crumbs falling from between her fingers onto the leather bench that she realized she'd crushed her cookie.

She grimaced, opening her hand to stare in dismay at the mess. Chocolate, even the kind in crappy mass-produced cookies, deserved more respect.

"Look, forget I asked, okay?" she blurted out, needing to fill the silence. "Obviously you've been running Can-Do for a long time and you know what works and what won't."

Like watching an ice cube melt in the hot sun, the taut line of his shoulders slowly eased and his face relaxed. Then he shrugged and looked away with a deep sigh.

"No. I'm the one who pushed the subject. Which means you deserve to have it answered."

Her mouth dropped.

"Who are you and what'd you do with Jason Cantrell?" she asked.

That dispelled the last of the tension. He laughed and reached over to take her crumb-filled hand. He locked his gaze on hers. His blue eyes filled with mischief as he turned her hand over to shake the crumbs into a napkin. Crumpling it, he then lifted her palm to his mouth and licked the melted chocolate from her skin.

His tongue was hot. Fire flamed low in her belly, making her suddenly damp lips tremble with need. His tongue slid fingers of her free hand into a fist, nails cutting into the skin, and tried to convince herself that jumping him was a really, really bad idea for a really long list of reasons.

They had no future.

She'd hate herself in the morning if she gave in to meaningless sex.

He'd walked away from her once already and broke her heart.

They didn't have a condom.

His tongue swirled over the soft, meaty flesh between her thumb and her forefinger, then he sucked softly.

Her list went up in flames as her brain shut down. Her breath shuddered, molten heat making her thighs damp. Two more seconds of this and she'd rip her own clothes off and climb all over him.

"I thought you were going to answer my question," she gasped.

His mouth paused its delectable torment to frown at her words. She used his hesitation to pull her hand away, tucking it under her hip to hide it until the tingling stopped.

The look of sexy mischief left his eyes just before Jason looked away. She winced, then told herself to stop being such a wimp. She wasn't trying to fix his business or find a way for him to stick around this time. She was just asking a simple question—one that he'd insisted he was going to answer. It wasn't like she was breaking any rules.

"Peter's going to get a regular job, sure," Jason finally said. "But he's like me. It'll drive him nuts after awhile. I know he thinks this is going to work out for him, the settling down and staying in one place. But it can't last."

"You're saying there is no way your brother, who loves this woman enough to marry her, will be happy spending his life with her?" Larissa snapped, knowing she was projecting but not caring. Unable to stay still, she started pacing the seven-foot distance between the bench and the storefront.

"You realize this isn't about us, right?" he chimed in, sounding bored as he leaned back, his elbows on the side of the bench.

"I'm just saying, how can a marriage work if one of the two people involved is going to be miserable? Wasn't it Peter who pointed out that little fact when we got engaged? Didn't he say that you'd hate being stuck and eventually hate me for making you stay around?" The words were bitter on her tongue. She stopped pacing to plant her fists on her hips and glare. "So how is it going to be different for Mr. Know It All? How is his marriage going to survive?"

"I don't give a shit what happens to Peter's marriage," Jason snapped, no longer looking relaxed as he sat up straight and returned her glare. "I need to make sure there is a large enough steady income to keep my mom in the assisted living home and off state assistance."

Larissa's anger drained so fast, it should have been accompanied by a sucking sound. Her cheeks warmed and her eyes burned. She hadn't known his mom was in a home. Iris Cantrell had had a stroke while on an archeological dig five years ago. Her husband had gotten her medical care as fast as possible, but she'd been permanently affected and unable to care for herself ever since. The last Larissa had known, Iris and Lawrence had retired here in South Carolina.

"I'm sorry. I didn't realize she was doing so poorly. I guess your dad can't take care of her on his own any longer?" Larissa asked quietly.

"Dad wasn't cut out to play nursemaid, apparently," Jason said, rising to take over her pacing track. "After her second stroke, she was a lot more dependent. Dad couldn't handle it. Right before we split up, actually, he filed for divorce. They never had much, since all their money went back into their research. He left her the house, but took what little cash they had."

Why hadn't he told her? Turned to her? Despite her own feeling of rejection, Larissa reached out a hand in support, wanting to offer something, anything, to ease the pain and anger in his voice. But his back was to her as he stared at the dark, empty wall of stores.

Before she could think of anything to say, he took a loud breath, then shrugged like he was shaking off his emotions. When he turned back to her, his face was calm. But she could still see the pain in his eyes.

"So that's why I need to keep Can-Do Adventures kicking ass. There are responsibilities. And for now, they fall to me to handle. Peter will be back full time eventually. That's not a reflection on his marriage, simply a fact. We Cantrell men are just made that way."

"And his wife?"

"Meghan's cool," Jason judged, looking uncomfortable. "I guess they've talked about it. She'll travel a little, too. She says she'll be okay with whatever Peter does."

Unlike Larissa.

It was a damned good thing she wasn't in love with Jason any longer. And just as soon as her heart stopped crumbling like that stupid cookie, she'd work on being grateful.

"So what about you?" Jason asked, rocking back on his heels, hands in his pockets, looking so casual that it would be easy to overlook his tight face and hunched shoulders. "You still haven't explained why you're still at the same bookstore. What happened to all your dreams? I can't believe you'd wait this long and change them that much."

His words poured out so fast, she knew he was using them like a shield. Like her advice, or even her company for anything more than a few weeks, Jason didn't want her sympathy.

She swallowed the ball of misery that'd welled up in her throat and made a show of gathering their dinner leftovers to hide her face so he wouldn't see the pain burning in her eyes.

"You're not going to share?" he asked after a painful silence.

"There isn't much to share," she said tonelessly as she

walked a few feet over to a trash can to toss everything, eaten or not. "I already told you that I'd decided to take some classes, solidify my foundation and perfect my business plan before I made a big move."

Shoulders knotted, she debated returning to the bench or finding somewhere to hide until she had a grip on her crazy, out-of-control emotions. But it was getting hotter by the minute, the air a physical thing now, like a heavy, damp blanket laying over the mall. If it was this warm out here in the open mall, she knew the heat would be worse hiding in the store.

"So you've spent the last two years going to school?" Jason prodded.

He wouldn't let her run and hide. He'd fessed up, and he would insist she do the same. So Larissa returned to the pool of candlelight surrounding the bench. She didn't sit, though.

"I've been building a foundation," she corrected. "I'm known as one of the leading authorities on romance in the country now."

His mouth dropped. Actually grateful for a way to break the emotional ice, she asked in a teasing tone. "What's with the shock? You don't think I'm qualified?"

He opened his mouth, then shut it and shrugged. "I have no idea. I don't even know what that means. Are you famous or something?"

She gave a little laugh. "Not famous, really. I started an online column a few years back called Romance Rules. It turned into a big hit. It was syndicated, then picked up by *Cosmopolitan* magazine."

Jason's eyes widened.

"I thought that was more about sex and fashion than hearts and flowers."

"I provide contrast and balance," she informed him with a

big smile. "Actually, I'm really proud of how well it's going. I was nervous at first. I mean, like you say, their platform is pretty much living the sexy life. But we quickly found out that even sexy lives need romance. Now I'm a hit."

She was proud of how she'd made that distinction. That women could have full, exciting sex lives that made them feel loved and wanted and needed. After all, that's what romance boiled down to in her opinion. Feeling special because of love.

"So you have all that going for you," he said with a proud grin. "That's great. I'm going to have to pick up one of those magazines and see what you're advising."

Larissa gave him a slow, shy smile. She'd had this secret fantasy once. Or twice. Or every time she wrote an article— that Jason might randomly pick up the magazine while waiting in an airport or doctors office and see her name. He'd be curious, then awed at her advice column. And he'd see all the things he'd done wrong in their relationship and hurry back to fix them.

A crazy fantasy. Especially since she knew he only read travel pieces and spy novels.

"But why open a store here if you've got that going on?" he asked. "If you're going to keep a store and that romance thing, I'd think you'd stay in the house the bookstore is already in. You always seemed to love that place."

She crashed back to earth with a mental thud as she realized his interest was really all about the store, not her.

"The Victorian is fine," she explained, her tone a little chilly. "It's gorgeous and wonderfully preserved. Mr. Murphy has even made a number of renovations based on my suggestions. The dining room and back parlor were combined to create a café. It does a nice amount of business, and there are four bookclubs that meet there monthly."

She babbled on for another few minutes about the glory

and wonder of Murphy's Books before she noticed the little smile on Jason's face.

Her voice trailed off as she struggled to read that smile. "What?" she asked.

"You love that store. I get it. What I don't get is why you're still there. You're a nationwide romance authority. You've got two degrees, what I'm sure is the best business plan in existence and unless you've gone crazy, you had a decent chunk of money to fund whatever plans you had."

"So?"

"So I'm confused. I asked you before but you haven't answered me. Why haven't you left the store to start your own gig long before this? Or why haven't you simply bought old man Murphy out, like you said you were going to two years ago and made that store your own?"

JASON WAS SURPRISED at how much he needed to know that answer. It wasn't like she'd been under contract to follow through with her plans, even though those damned plans had been a major player in their breakup.

"As wonderful as it is, it doesn't fit the image I want to create," she confessed, sitting on the bench and giving him a dreamy sort of look. "A dedicated bookstore is a wonderful thing, but I don't want to focus solely on books. I want to expand to all things romantic. That's the name of my store, by the way, Isn't It Romantic."

"Cute." And it was. In a fluffy, girly kind of way. From a guy's angle, she'd bet it was a little hive-inducing. "So it's a girl store? I'd have thought females would swoon over Murphy's place. It's got all that quaint architecture and history and character. But if you don't want to do it there, why not open in a typical mall?"

His *why here?* was unspoken but clear.

"The Victorian is in a smaller neighborhood and brings in local patrons but won't ever get the kind of foot traffic The Cartright will bring in," she said, looking around the space like she was seeing it filled with rich shoppers, their fists filled with credit cards as they stampeded toward her doors. "This location will not only bring in guest shoppers from all over the country, but the local businesses will patronize it as well. The median income of the shoppers here will be much higher than the average mall, too."

He frowned. Was he the only one who saw the glitch in her plan?

"Don't take this wrong, but these stores…" He waved his hand to indicate the closed doors lining the mall walkway. "Tiffany, Louis Vuitton, Apple. These are all pretty high dollar, right?"

"So?" she snapped. "Isn't that why you want to make a sex museum here? To attract the high dollar customers?"

"It's not a sex museum," he corrected with a grin, glad she remembered his plans. "It's an opportunity to partake in exclusive couples' weekend adventures."

"Whatever," she dismissed. "This place is perfect for all the reasons I've already told you. And clearly, my window display would look better next to Tiffany's glitter than your penis stick."

His grin widened. She had a good point. Not that he'd give up his claim, but that koteka was a pretty beat up piece of wood. Propping it in a window next to a bunch of diamonds was a little pathetic.

"Regardless of which one of our windows would look better next to the diamonds, I'm still confused."

"About?"

"Daniel told me they'd just made the decision to hold one space for a local friend a month ago. You couldn't have been planning on this location for all that time."

Larissa's smile faded. She looked down at her skirt, brushing at the fabric like she was trying to smooth out the wrinkles with her palm.

"I'd get it if you'd opened at a different location and were looking to move up," he said. "But you're just getting rolling. So what's the deal? Why the delay in starting your own business?"

She'd always used the store as a reason not to travel with him.

Had it all been bullshit?

Had all those middle-of-the-night doubts about his career choice been brought on by a lie?

"I told you—"

"Right," he interrupted. "You had to build a stronger foundation. Which sounds great. But that's not what you said you were going to do a couple of years ago." When they'd broke up over it, dammit. "You said you needed to focus on getting your shit together so you could buy Murphy's store."

She clamped her arms across her belly. He wondered if she knew her jacket was still unbuttoned enough to make that move a gorgeous temptation as the candlelight flickered over the curves of her breasts.

Jason tore his gaze away, forcing himself to keep his eyes on her face. That's where he'd find answers. Looking for them in the other parts of her body only led to trouble.

"I didn't buy the store right after we split up because…" She stared past his shoulder for a second like she was trying to figure out exactly what to say. Or how to say it. Then she gave a little one-shouldered shrug that played havoc on his intention to keep his eyes on her face. "I wasn't in a good place, emotionally, after we split up. It took me awhile to be sure of myself. Of my dream. I'd already lost one of the most important things in my life. I didn't want to blow the other."

Jason winced. He'd have rather she kicked him in the gut with those high heels of hers. He hated that he'd hurt her, even though she'd been the one to cheat. Yeah, he might have mentally called her all manner of horrible names at the time, but that didn't mean he hadn't known that she had to have been miserable with him if she was going to do something that drastic. Before, he'd have sworn that cheating wasn't in Larissa's repertoire.

But he'd been so pissed, so worried he'd do something violent, he'd walked off when she'd refused to explain. So this was the first chance he'd had to deal with the aftermath of their breakup, face to face.

It didn't feel any better now than it would have then.

Obviously uncomfortable with sharing as much as she had—or with his pained silence—Larissa sprang to her feet. Before she could go anywhere, he stepped forward, blocking her path. He didn't know what he wanted to say to her. Hell, he didn't even know what he wanted from her. A chance to worship her body for a few hours, sure. But she wasn't the type of girl to offer up a free ride. And he wouldn't have… liked her as much if she were. From the time they were kids, he'd had a thing for her. But he'd ignored it. Mostly because of just that reason. Larissa was a good girl.

Which was why he'd asked her to marry him. Because a guy didn't do all those lustful and wild things to a good girl unless he planned to do right by her, too.

He'd have probably done them both a favor if he'd just seduced her without offering up a lot of promises he'd known he couldn't keep.

"Jason, I'd like to pass, please," she said quietly.

"Wait a second," he said. He still didn't know what to say. He just knew he had to say something.

So he spoke from the heart. Or somewhere close by.

"Look, we both made mistakes before. But, you know, I miss you," he admitted quietly. Her eyes rounded so wide, her lush eyelashes almost touched her brows.

Taking that as a good sign, Jason stepped closer, trailing one finger along the smooth skin of her cheek before slipping his knuckle under her chin to lift her face to his.

She didn't slap him away. Another good sign.

"I'm not claiming monkhood or anything, but I haven't had a relationship since we split," he confessed. "I've never found anyone I wanted to be with like I want you. Never cared about anyone else enough to want to spend the time or effort to build something."

Her tongue slipped out to wet her lips, making his fingers clench. She stared into his eyes as if she were trying to see into his soul. He shifted, a little uncomfortable at that idea. After all, even he didn't know what was in there.

"So? What do you think?" he asked, cringing inwardly at his awkwardness. He'd had more finesse in grade school. But that look on Larissa's face, so searching and honest, made him fumble.

"Think? About what, exactly?"

"About us. You and me. Spending some time together," he clarified, starting to regain his verbal footing. "After we're out of here, I mean."

She blinked a couple times, a tiny wrinkle forming between her eyebrows. Tilting her head to one side, she asked, "Like...what? Dating?"

"Right," he said, relieved that she'd waded through his fumbling to get to the heart of his suggestion. "Date, hang out, get cozy."

He slid his hand around to cup her chip, marveling at how soft her skin was beneath his fingers. Leaning down, he held her eyes as he brushed a whisper soft kiss over her lips.

The frown didn't go away, though.

"What do you think?" he asked, trying a second kiss, this one with a little more pressure.

She moved her head back. Just enough to break contact with his mouth. She didn't pull her chin from his hand, though. That was a good sign, right?

"So you want to go back to what we had before, without the commitment. We date. When you're in town. We hang out. When you have time. And we get cozy. When you're horny."

Jason narrowed his eyes. Was she pissed? He couldn't read her tone. Her face was blank.

"We can get cozy when you're horny, too," he promised trying out his most charming smile.

She didn't smile back.

"Well?" he encouraged. He knew he should wait. He should have been more tactful, maybe a little more seductive. He should have started by asking for a date, not lining it all up like that.

But still, maybe she'd say yes.

Holding his breath, he waited. Larissa gave him a long, indecipherable look. The she slowly shook her head. Shoulders low, she pressed her lips together before saying, "I don't think it'd be a good idea. I doubt either one of us has changed what we want out of life. Or out of a relationship. So why go through the misery and disappointment all over again?"

"It doesn't have to be misery if we know from the get go what the game plan is," Jason objected, even though he knew she was right. But, dammit, he didn't want her to be. He wanted it all. His career and freedom. And the woman he...cared a great deal about.

He winced, knowing if she could hear his thoughts she'd give him that arched look of hers as if to say, see, *I told you so.*

"I need a break," she said, looking around, flustered.

"And what do you suggest I do while you hole up in the store?" he snapped, even though he knew he was more angry with himself than her.

She bent gracefully and lifted the candle, then handed it to him.

"Why don't you go explore the mall, or break into the hotel or even try climbing the walls to find a way out of here. If it helps, pretend I agreed to another of your non-committal relationships. That should inspire you fast enough."

# 9

LARISSA WANTED TO PAT HERSELF on the back.

She hadn't kicked Jason in the balls like she'd wanted.

She hadn't thrown anything when she stepped into the softly lit store.

And she hadn't screamed. At least, she hadn't until she'd reached the bathroom at the very back of the store. And then she did her screaming into the blanket she'd grabbed on her way back.

All things considered, it was an excellent show of self-control.

That she'd been locked in the bathroom for ten minutes and couldn't bring herself to go back out might not be so brave. But dammit, it wasn't every day a girl had an invitation for a romance-less, non-committal, non-relationship filled with lots of hot, steamy sex.

She closed her eyes and leaned her forehead against the cool door, breathing in the faint scent of fresh paint.

"Maybe if I hide in here long enough, Jason will actually find an escape route," she muttered. Or maybe, hopefully, she'd overcome the urge to run out there, throw herself in his arms and agree to anything he wanted as long as she was the only girl he was cozying up with.

What'd she said to Chloe just this afternoon? That she didn't believe in gratuitous sex. That without emotion and commitment, sex was a shallow thing. What kind of evil universe did she live in that it'd test her like this?

"Chloe's gonna laugh her ass off when she hears about this," Larissa told herself. "And probably suggest I get therapy when she hears I'm having conversations with myself."

Finally, more because she didn't want Jason to come looking for her and find her hiding in a bathroom than any sense of bravery or ability to handle the situation, she turned the doorknob. Taking her flickering candle, she returned to the damply humid darkness of the store, looking around as she went.

No Jason.

She went to the arched entrance and held her candle high.

No Jason.

She thought about calling out. But she didn't want him back that badly.

His penis box was still tucked under the bench, though, so she figured he hadn't escaped yet.

Not caring if an ax murderer showed up this time, she set her candle on the checkout counter and looked around. She needed to distract herself or she'd go insane. She pulled her briefcase over and emptied the contents so she could sort and tidy it, figuring there had to be something in here she could work on.

An hour later, she'd revised her brochure, noting in the margins changes she'd like to make. She'd written a thank you letter to Conner, Ben and Franklin, accepting their imaginarily generous offer. She pulled out her business plan, intending to go through and revise it now that she'd spent time—*way too much time*—in the actual store space.

She had to admit, she was a little intimidated by the stature of the stores around her. Could she pull this off? Was *Isn't It Romantic* a big enough idea to justify her spot in this mall?

"Sure it is. You're one of a kind. You're in *Cosmo,* for crying out loud," she assured herself. Besides, what was it Conner had suggested?

"Romance à la Cartright?" She wrinkled her nose. "Stupid idea."

That wasn't part of the deal, was it? She jotted down a note to make sure he'd been joking. But it was flattering to be asked, right? That proved she was a strong enough contender for the space.

"Not like some travel agency," she muttered.

She flipped through the pages of her business plan. But she couldn't concentrate.

Where the hell was Jason?

Larissa looked around, but there was no sign of life in the dark emptiness beyond her doorway. She listened, but could only hear a pounding splatter of rain hitting the mall entry windows.

She breathed in the muggy air. If she had to be trapped like this, she wished there could have at least been a little window somewhere she could open to ventilate some of this hot air out.

Was he coming back?

Not that she cared, really. But if he wasn't, she could take off her jacket and skirt and curl up on the cool marble floor to get comfortable.

Leave it to Jason to make being trapped without electricity or outside contact even more miserable. Thoroughly disgusted with the entire situation, she tossed her notebook and pen down. They slid across the counter, stopping just short of toppling off the other side.

"This is ridiculous."

Larissa bit her lip, trying to decide what to do. She picked up the almost-burned down candle and walked to the door, looking out to the right, then the left.

No Jason.

She shrugged. She'd be damned if she'd call for him.

And she was dying of heat exhaustion here.

Trying to ignore the tiny skitter of fear tracking up and down her spine, she turned back into the store and considered. Then, looking over her shoulder again to make sure Jason hadn't sneaked up behind her, she made quick work of what was left of her jacket's buttons. She shrugged it off, then looked around and hung it from one of the wall sconces so the silk wouldn't wrinkle any worse.

She bent down to unbuckle the straps of her darling red patent-leather mary-janes, sighing in pleasure as she slipped her sweaty feet out of the tight shoes. She wiggled her toes a few times, then planted her feet flat on the floor, trying to absorb some of the coolness from the chilly stone.

Close, but she wasn't quite comfortable yet.

Nerves giving her goose bumps despite the heat, she hurried back to the doorway to look around again. No sign of Jason's candle or Jason himself.

Not that it mattered. She'd told him to take a hike and she was sure he would. He'd never stuck around to fight for their relationship when it'd mattered. So why would he hang around to argue for some random cozy times now?

"No obsessing," she chided herself.

Then, one eye on the door, she quickly shimmied out of her skirt. She sighed in pleasure as the air, even as moist and warm as it was, cooled her legs.

She wrapped the blanket around her hips, tucking in one end of the fluffy fabric to hold it in place. Not the perfect answer, but definitely more comfortable than her skirt and this way her modesty was safe.

She glanced at her lace and satin covered breasts and shrugged. Okay, so her modesty was *almost* safe.

Not that it mattered. "He's probably gnawed his way through a wall somewhere and is hightailing it off to the Amazon by now."

Sick and crazy with the constant silence, Larissa looked around. She had a stack of mood music CDs in her box of goodies. But nothing to play them on.

Needing noise, she started humming as she squatted down by the box to flip through the CDs.

"Hmm, hmm, *time for me to go home,*" she hummed. *"Getting late, dark outside."*

She set the CDs aside and pulled out the variety of Chloe's specialty boxes she'd brought to display. Even in the dim candlelight, the packaging screamed romance. Embossed lettering, shiny ribbon and gold foil stripes. Pretty.

*"I need to be with myself,"* she continued to sing quietly as she pried open one box labeled *Sweet Sensuality.* *"Clarity, peace, serenity."*

Into her hands poured the makings of a very romantic, very sexy evening. Chocolate body paint, love dice, fluffy feathers on a stick, a very ambitious number of condoms and yet another candle. Larissa didn't have to lift the glass jar to her nose to know what scent it was. Black Cherry Vanilla wafted around her.

She closed her eyes. She hadn't smelled that in years. It'd been her favorite, the scent she'd always lit for her romantic evenings with Jason.

Beginning with their first night together. After years of secretly crushing on him, pretending to be happy being just a friend, Jason had finally asked her out. She'd seen it as her very own romance novel, albeit a very sexy one. She'd worn a tiny excuse for a dress, one that had narrow straps and a beaded bodice that let her go braless.

The night, and Jason, had been straight out of a romance novel. They'd gone to dinner. They'd hit the clubs and danced. They'd barely drank, already intoxicated on each other. And when Jason had walked her to the door, she'd invited him in. And lit her candle.

And, while he got comfortable on the couch thinking he was going to get a snack, she'd stripped naked. And given him a whole lot more to eat.

It'd been the beginning of her very own fairy tale. Her hot, sexy prince had swept her off her feet. The sex… Larissa fanned her hand in front of her face, feeling her skin heat up. The sex had been incredible. Better, even, than all the romance novel sex she'd ever read about.

But it'd been all flash and no substance. Not real romance. Because even then, when things had been so incredible, she'd known it wouldn't—couldn't—last. That he wouldn't stick around.

She glanced at the goodies in her hand, regretting for an instant that as great as the sex had been, they'd never gotten naughty. No chocolate body paint, no whipped cream bikini, no kinky games.

Who knew how much more incredible sex could have been with a little adventure added in? Maybe if Jason had actually loved her, had trusted her, they'd have had a chance to find out.

If he'd trusted her, he wouldn't have thought twice about her dinner with Conner. She'd done it hundreds of times before they were engaged. Why would she stop simply because she and Jason were a couple? It hadn't been anything other than two friends having a meal. Granted, the meal had been on Conner's yacht, but that was just a Conner thing.

She'd been such an idiot. Even after their huge breakup

fight, when Jason had accused her of all kinds of ugliness with Conner, she'd hoped—believed—that he'd come back to her.

That's how it always happened in the books. But he hadn't. Jason had hit the road, obviously thrilled to be free and unencumbered again. She'd waited. And waited. But he hadn't returned.

Finally, she'd had to accept that he really wasn't her hero, after all. Or that she wasn't romance material.

Hence, the birth of her romance rules. Because with a solid outline, she could make sure her next relationship was one she could count on.

"He's just the guy who broke my heart," she murmured, standing carefully, as if moving too fast would set off a crying jag. Larissa set the candle and the rest of the goodies back in the box. All, except the condoms. She stared at that string of possibilities, the images of her and Jason's naked body wrapped around each other flashing through her head.

She fingered the condoms, her thumb sliding over the slick foil. She should leave them in the box. She should put them back in the planter out front. Better yet, flush them all down the toilet so they wouldn't tempt her.

She swallowed, trying to calm her racing pulse.

"That looks a lot more comfortable."

Larissa's scream echoed through the almost empty room. The string of condoms flew out of her hand. She was glad she was barefoot, since she jumped at least a foot high before spinning around. Her fist clutched the blanket to keep it from coming loose.

This time Jason didn't laugh at her reaction. He just set his almost gutted candle on the counter next to hers and waited for her to regain her composure.

"Where'd you come from?" she asked as soon as her

voice worked again. It was like he'd been conjured up by her horny thoughts.

"A twinkle in my daddy's eye," he said. His words were light, but he sounded tired.

"I've heard twinkles are dangerous," she said slowly, trying to read his expression in the dim light. Something was…off. She didn't know what was wrong with him, but something was. It wasn't like he'd be upset over her turning down his oh-so-romantic proposal, so it had to be something else.

The sight of him, so sexy as he stood in the doorway, made her melt a little. Was it wrong to want one more memory? To want a little of that adventurous sex to remember him by?

"Twinkles are usually nothing but trouble," he confirmed as he stepped farther into the store. He shoved his hands into the front pockets of his jeans and looked around.

Larissa looked around, too, trying to figure out what he was seeing. Then she stepped closer. His furrowed brow and down-turned lips made her want to give him a hug.

She waited for him to say something else. Anything else.

Silence. She was so freaking tired of silence.

Finally, she couldn't stand it. She hated seeing him hurting. So she laid a hand on his arm and asked, "What's the matter?"

His wince was infinitesimal, so small that if she hadn't been touching him, she wouldn't have caught it.

"Nothing."

"Right," she agreed. "That's why you look like someone just shredded your passport."

He didn't even crack a smile.

"Did you find out we're really stuck here all weekend?" she asked, panicking a little. Not so much at the idea of being trapped for the entire weekend—was there enough food or would they have to resort to the body paint? No, what really scared her was how appealing the idea suddenly was.

"Nah. Like I said, Conner will be here before noon tomorrow."

Larissa pursed her lips, then decided that circumstances justified calling out the big guns.

She stepped a little closer, not touching him but close enough to feel the heat radiating off his body.

She gave a deep sigh, knowing the move would challenge the lace of her camisole.

And she gave him the look. Chin down, puppy dog eyes through the fringe of her lashes and her lower lip protruding just a little.

He burst out laughing. "God, that's pathetic."

"Got you to laugh, though," Larissa pointed out with a grin. Tucking her hair behind her ear, she tilted her head and asked quietly, "Seriously. What's wrong?"

"I guess I need to apologize," he finally muttered. He dropped his gaze, staring at her bare toes instead of her face.

Larissa couldn't have been more shocked if he'd announced he was planning a sex change operation. Or, to be honest, more horrified. Jason never apologized. He'd never felt he'd done anything that warranted saying the word "sorry."

But he did now? What had he done that she didn't know about? She thought of all those nights he'd spent away from her and her heart whimpered.

Suddenly she realized how blindsided and miserable he must have felt when he thought she'd cheated on him with Conner. It was like someone was ripping her guts out through her heart.

"Why?" she said when she found her voice.

"We never should have gotten engaged. I should have known it'd end like it did."

Anger slowly seeped through her bloodstream. Even though she'd had a million doubts herself, it still infuriated her to hear that Jason hadn't had any faith in them.

So pissed she was surprised steam wasn't pouring out her ears, Larissa slapped her arms over her chest and tilted her chin. "Really? Why? How were we doomed to failure?"

"Not us. Me."

Her steam sputtered.

"I thought there were two of us in that relationship."

"Yeah, but you're not all messed up."

"And…" She shook her head, really confused. Jason had always been the epitome of confidence. What had happened? "What messed you up?"

"My father."

Wincing, Larissa remembered his earlier confession about his father walking out on his mom. Jason had always identified with his father. And, on the surface, the men were a lot alike. Charming and easygoing. Upbeat and friendly. But underneath, Louis Cantrell had seemed more focused on his own goals, his own plans, than the good of anyone else. Unlike Jason, who seemed to put his entire family before his own wants.

"You're not your father, Jason."

"I'm his son. You know as well as anyone how like him I am," he countered. His words held a bitterness she'd never heard before. "Hell, aren't we the perfect example of just how much like him I am? I hurt you like he hurt my mom. What's the diff?"

"The difference is that you are the one who's taking care of your mom." She risked her own peace of mind to offer the small comfort of laying her hand on his warm, muscled arm. God, he felt good. Swallowing, she forced herself to continue. "You were faced with the same choices as your dad, but you went a different route. Even now, you're willing to sideline your own goals to make sure your family is taken care of. Your dad never did that. Do you think, when you were kids, that he'd have stayed home if you boys couldn't go on digs with him?"

Jason's brow creased, then he gave a sigh.

"Probably not," he muttered. "But that doesn't mean I'm not like him."

Unable to help herself, she patted his arm again. The muscles were hard and inviting beneath her fingers. He looked like the sexiest thing to wear jeans. He sounded like a hurt little boy. He was the strongest man she knew, and the most caring.

She really, really wished she could think he was the jerk he now thought his father was. Then dismissing her feelings for him would be easier. Leftover feelings, sure. Just a little unfinished business, she assured herself. A little hot, sexy unfinished business.

Larissa sighed. She looked away, giving herself a second to make sure she wasn't about to make a huge mistake.

Did it matter, though? She wanted this. She missed this so much. So if it was a mistake, well, she'd just add it to the rest of the things she regretted about her and Jason.

She looked at him again. The shadows painted dark slashes and angles on his face, showing her depths she'd never realized he had. Depths she wished she didn't know about now, since they only added to his appeal. Since she'd already read their romance story, she knew how it ended.

She knew she was crazy to want to open those pages again. But she didn't care.

JASON FOUGHT THE URGE to turn and run from the room. He couldn't believe he'd told her his dirty little secret. He'd come back to make sure she was set for the night before he found a corner to crash in. Not to dump all his emotional crap at her feet.

And he definitely hadn't figured it for a ploy to play his way back into her good graces.

But he couldn't move. The soft pressure of her hand on his arm was as effective a trap as those big-ass locks holding them inside the building.

"Our doom aside, do you really think your parents had a horrible relationship?" she asked, her tone making it clear she was humoring his melodrama. "Despite the rotten way your father left, didn't your parents have almost thirty years together that didn't suck?"

Jason frowned. "What difference does that make? Those thirty years were easy times. He couldn't hack being there when it counted."

"And I thought I was the 'all or nothing' romantic in this relationship," she said with a small shake of her head. She lifted her hand off his arm, leaving him chilled and lonely. She gave him a long, considering look. Like she was already regretting whatever she was about to do.

Then, tightening the knot of her blanket, she hitched her fluffy bastion of modesty a little higher and turned, giving him a tempting view of the silky skin of her back and smooth shoulders.

He wanted to touch her. To slide his hands over her skin and lose himself in the welcoming warmth of her body. He hated all this emotional crap. Drama should stay on the big screen, not foist itself on real life. At least, not on his life.

Resigned, Jason watched Larissa walk away. He should be used to seeing the back of her by now. But she didn't retreat into whatever hidey-hole she'd claimed in the back-room. He frowned, watching her slowly pace the far wall, staring at the floor like she was searching for something.

He glanced down, but couldn't see a thing. The darkness swallowed her feet, making her look like she was floating in that blanket. Apparently she found it, though, because she knelt down and swept her hand across the floor.

He frowned, trying to make out what it was. She tucked her hand into the folds of her blanket, though, as she made her way back across the room to stop inches from him.

His body heated, his mind went blank for just a second as her scent wrapped around him in the warm air. His fingers itched to touch her. His mouth watered to taste her. His dick...well, it went without saying what it wanted to do. Same thing it always wanted whenever Larissa was around.

Looking as heartbreakingly serious as she had the night she'd told him they were over, Larissa stared into his eyes. Jason swallowed. He'd broken his arm when he was a kid riding his bike. Then, years later, he'd rebroke it in the same place. It hadn't hurt any less the second time around.

He wasn't in love with Larissa. He couldn't be. Wouldn't let himself be. But damned if he wanted his heart kicked a second time around.

He tried to think of something to say to shift the mood. A joke or clever comment. But before he could come up with anything, she held out her hand.

Jason winced before he remembered that she couldn't be holding his ring again, she'd given that back once already.

He looked down. He blinked, giving his head a little shake to reengage his brain.

Even in the flickering candlelight, the foil shape was unmistakable.

"A condom?" he asked, still needing confirmation.

She opened her fingers, letting a string of at least a dozen of those little rubber beauties trail over her palm.

He grinned at her faith in his prowess. Damned if he wouldn't do his best not to let her down.

"If this is a dream," he begged, as he took the foil-wrapped keys to heaven, "don't wake me up."

"How about I keep you up?" she offered with a teasingly wicked little smile.

The sight of that look, her sparkling eyes and sweet smirk, was like a punch in the gut. He hadn't realized how much he'd missed that look. Missed her. Until now.

"I thought you said you didn't want to do the cozy friends with benefits thing," he reluctantly reminded her. His dick throbbed in protest. Like it wanted to scream out, no! We're so close, don't blow it.

The wicked look left her face, leaving a bittersweet smile. She tilted her head so a curtain of black curls swept across her shoulder, brushing the lace of her camisole.

"That's not what this is. I'm not opening the door to a future between us, even a cozy non-committed one." She touched a finger to the foil wrappers. "I know we can't be what each other needs. But for right now, right here, we can be what each other wants."

"And that's enough?"

"It can be," she said quietly.

"So this is just for the night?"

"Tonight," she confirmed. "Or as long as the condoms last."

Jason fought a frown. A part of him—a part he didn't even recognize—wanted to scream *hell, no*. Maybe they had no future, given all their issues. But what was between them was more than easy sex.

Maybe he had issues with commitment, but what he and Larissa had been to each other had been pretty damn special. Too special to cheapen with a night of rolling around in an empty building lust.

He stared into her dark eyes, trying to read what was going through her head. This was just what he'd wanted. To be with her without the pressure and expectations and guilt. To enjoy the incredible intensity of their passion.

And she was offering it up, commitment-free.

Why did that feel so wrong?

Telling himself to quit being a dork, Jason gave in to his body's demands. The tips of his fingers caressed her bare shoulder, reveling in the silken texture of her skin. He bent his head, pressing his lips to that same spot and breathing in her delicious scent.

"Then we'd better get to it, then," he said, his voice husky with desire as he tossed the foil wrappers onto the counter, in easy reach. "We've got a lot of condoms to go through."

# 10

Jason lost himself in the taste of Larissa's mouth. Their lips slid together, soft and sweet. He loved how her fingers dug into his shoulders. Like she couldn't get enough.

A part of him, the part quickly getting drowned out, wished they had a chance for more. Wished she'd agreed to give his idea a chance. If she was willing to have one night of commitment-free fun, why not a bunch of nights?

But if all he could get was this night, he'd make damned sure it was one she never forgot.

With that in mind, he swept his tongue over her lips in a gentle caress. She tasted so sweet, so tempting. He wanted to keep it gentle, to build and tease. But her warmth pulled him in.

He nipped at her lower lip, a gentle little bite. Her gasp gave him entrance to her mouth. Lips sliding together, their tongues danced a hot, fast rhythm.

He rolled her nipple between his thumb and forefinger, loving how she shuddered in pleasure. He'd climbed mountains, jumped from planes and rappelled down cliffs. But nothing made him feel more manly than the response Larissa gave him. He scraped his thumbnail over the turgid tip of her breast, making her moan.

He wanted to climb inside her, to be a part of her and hear her not just moan, but scream his name. He wanted it so bad, he was afraid he'd do anything, say anything and definitely promise any damned thing, just to have her.

Which was what had gotten him in trouble before.

Remembering, Jason forced himself to slow down. He softened the kiss until they were barely nibbling at each other's lips, then shifted to her cheek before taking a slow, meandering journey down her throat.

Yeah. He was still in control. It was all good.

He breathed in her scent, made all the stronger in the dark for some reason. Spicy sweet and sexy as hell.

Control, Cantrell, he lectured. Keep it light and fun.

"I can't believe you carry condoms," he said, laughing against her shoulder. "I have to admit, it doesn't quite jive with the romance authority image I had in my head."

"There's nothing romantic about getting all riled up and having to quit just before the payoff," she reminded him as she swept her fingers up, then down his spine in a way that made him want to arch his back and purr like a cat.

"Speaking from recent experience, I'd have to agree," he said with a low laugh.

Her hand slipped lower, nails scraping gently at the small of his back through his shirt. He automatically shifted his pelvis forward, pressing his erection into her belly.

"So what other secrets are you keeping as the romance authority?" he teased, pressing little kisses down her arm until he reached her wrist. He took her hand in his and turned it over to place a warm, moist kiss in the center of her palm. He smiled when her fingers trembled in his.

"What makes you think I have secrets?" she breathed.

"All women have secrets." He lifted her knuckles to his lips, then pressed her hand flat against his belly. Her fingers slid between the buttons of his shirt, teasing his stomach.

"If I do," she told him after a just-a-beat-too-long pause. "Then they're obviously more romantic to keep to myself."

He wondered what she'd really wanted to say, then told himself it didn't matter. They were in for a night of incredible physical intimacy. They definitely didn't want to delve into that emotional intimacy crap.

"You would know, since you're the romance authority," he mused. "That sounds serious. Like you're in charge. You're obviously not wearing leather panties."

"That doesn't mean I won't take charge," she said.

Jason stopped kissing her throat long enough to give her a grin.

"What?" she asked.

"I'm not saying you're passive or anything, sweetheart. But I know your moves, remember."

"Is that so?"

"It is."

"Well, we'll just see about that," she promised, stepping out of his arms. "My turn, hotshot."

Grinning, Jason stepped back and raised both hands in surrender. He also knew which buttons to push. All it took was a hint that she was a little too sweet and Larissa would insist on proving him wrong. To his never-ending delight.

His grin dimmed a little as she turned away with a swirl of that fuzzy covering of hers, giving him a fluffy covered view of her behind when she bent over that box she'd hauled in.

When she turned back, she had a candle in one hand, which didn't much interest him except to ensure he could still see her as they pleasured each other. But the jar in her other hand...

His jaw dropped. Heat pounded a beat in his head as he

realized what she was holding. He thought she'd drop the blanket and start stripping his shirt off.

Talk about hitting the jackpot.

"Body paint?" he confirmed, squinting at the label. "We're having a little preloving snack?"

"Not we."

His brow arched. She set the candle on the counter, then with a flick of her fingers, let the blanket fall to the floor. Her body glowed as the golden light shimmered off her tiny little panties and satiny lace top.

Jason's blood poured out of his head. His breath shuddered and his mouth went dry.

"Just me?" he pleaded.

With a naughty look, she shook her head. Then she took the cootie matches and lit her new candle. A rich aroma instantly filled the air. Already turned on, Jason's dick got painfully hard at the smell. It was the scent of lovemaking. Of him and Larissa. Hot. Wild. Intense.

She set the chocolate over the candle flame, balancing it on the edges of the jar.

"How long will it take to get hot?"

"It's going to get hot fast," she promised. He shifted, trying to ease the stranglehold his jeans had on his pride.

As good as her word, Larissa stepped in front of him, using her fingernails to lightly scrape her way down his chest to his belly. Jason sucked in his gut. With a hard tug, she pulled his shirt from the waistband of his jeans and made quick work of the buttons. He shrugged it off, then reached out to wrap one hand around her waist to pull her closer as his other closed over the soft weight of her breast.

Before he could have too much fun, though, she pulled out of his arms. She gave him a teasing look and wiggled her brows, making her look like a naughty little fairy.

"Nope, no distracting me," she chided. "I'm hungry."

"I'm hungry, too," he countered with a laugh, anticipation building higher as she checked the jar of chocolate. She gave it a quick swirl, but apparently wasn't satisfied since she set it back over the flame.

"Isn't there some saying about ladies first?" she asked, walking back to him with a sexy little strut that made his mouth water. Her legs glowed gold in the light, the silky fabric of her camisole sliding temptingly over her breasts and emphasizing her tiny waist.

"You came first earlier," he added with a wicked grin.

"Well, now I get to return that favor," she promised.

She reached out to tap her fingernail on his buckle. Jason sucked in a breath, anticipating her next move and waiting for her to unhook the belt. But she didn't. Instead she scraped her fingernail over his zipper, making his already straining erection hit concrete hardness in a heartbeat.

"Strip," she ordered softly.

She looked so sweet. She sounded so innocent. It took him three seconds for her words to penetrate.

"Me, strip?"

"You. Strip for me."

His mouth went dry. He wasn't big on performances, other than the ones he could do between her legs.

He eyed the stubborn tilt of her chin and the impish look in her dark eyes and knew she would insist. And he'd thought her innocent? That romance authority thing was definitely going to her head.

Feeling like a Chippendales reject, Jason grimaced, then unbuckled his belt. Just as his fingers unsnapped his jeans, Larissa hummed a little bump and grind ditty low in her throat.

"Shit," he muttered. Then, seeing the amusement in her eyes, he grinned. She hummed some more. Picking up the beat, he jacked his hips to the left and unzipped. Jacked his hips to the right and kicked off his right shoe. Back to the left for the other shoe.

Stopping to awkwardly yank off his socks, he grinned when Larissa's mood music took on a quicker tempo. When he straightened, though, she slowed it back down to the traditional stripping beat.

"Where'd you learn that tune?" he asked.

"I'll tell you after you're naked," she promised, her words low and husky.

There was nothing to do but go for it, then. He slid his fingers under the waistband of his jeans, catching his boxers as well, and pushed, making sure he didn't damage the star of the show as he went.

With a quick kick, he shucked the pants off his legs and, getting into the moment, did an awkward dance move that was something between the Macarena without the hand moves and an electric slide.

"A dancer, I'm not," he said when he faced her again.

"You're the best naked dancer I've ever seen," she said, giggling a little.

"Isn't this where you slip a dollar into my G-string?" he asked with a laugh when she clapped.

"You're not wearing one," she replied, her words a purr of approval. She lifted the jar of chocolate and gave it a swirl, then offered him a big smile. "But I can paint one on for you."

Jason stopped laughing.

His pulse sped up, desire coiling tight at the thought of how she'd look licking that chocolate off his body. Of how he'd feel.

She uncapped the jar and stepped closer. The scent of milk chocolate, rich and sweet, filled the room. His mouth watered.

Then she dipped her finger into the jar. With her eyes locked on his, she placed her chocolate covered digit into her mouth and sucked. Jason almost exploded. His erection throbbed against his bare belly, begging for attention.

With two fingers, she scooped out more chocolate. Then, with a smile that made her look like a wickedly naughty fairy, she wiped the chocolate down his chest. The warm sticky liquid dripped, but Jason didn't look at it. His eyes were riveted on her.

She dipped again, this time painting the chocolate across his belly. Jason sucked in a breath, his heart pounding a loud rhythm in his head. He waited, desperately hoping.

She didn't disappoint him. Larissa's fourth foray into the chocolate jar covered four fingers. She released his gaze as her eyes dropped down his body. He followed her movements, watching her hand as she wrapped the warm treat around his throbbing cock.

Like she wasn't driving him insane, she concentrated on rubbing the chocolate over the rounded knob, then sliding her fingers up his shaft, then back down. Jason swallowed a groan. She swirled another layer of the rapidly cooling dessert over the head of his erection as if it needed double-dipping goodness.

She stepped closer, so close she was almost, but not quite, pressed against him. She gave him a wink, then nibbled licking little bites of the sweet confection off his chest. Jason sighed with pleasure.

He curved his fingers over her breasts, loving the weight, the soft cushion of them in his hands as she tasted her way over his chest. She shifted, nibbling lower. He watched her through slitted eyes, as turned on by the look of delight on her flushed face as he was by what she was doing to his body.

When she dropped to her knees in front of him, Jason was pretty sure he'd just died and was about to see heaven.

Then she blew on his dick. Warm air swirled around it. The feeling of her breath and the hardening chocolate made him groan out loud. He tunneled his fingers into her hair, needing to hold on. Needing to feel like he had some kind of control.

She leaned forward, her pink tongue licking him like there was no tomorrow. He shuddered. She cupped his butt with both of her hands, going to town on the chocolate as she sucked, nibbled and licked him clean. Jason was pretty sure he'd pass out if she didn't stop soon. Pass out or explode all over her. And he had other plans for his explosion.

Desperately, he tightened his fingers in her curls and pulled her head back.

"My turn," he insisted.

LARISSA RELUCTANTLY LET Jason pull her to her feet, licking bits of chocolate off her lips as she rose. Sweetness filled her mouth, desire burned through her body. She leaned forward to nibble at the chocolate still smeared on his chest, starving for his taste and unwilling to be deprived of a single bite.

He didn't give her time for more than a nibble, though. Apparently at his limit, he swung her into his arms, then kicked the blanket out flat on the floor before kneeling down on it.

His arms still holding her tight, Jason kissed her. Hot and wild, it was like he was starving. For her. Larissa's heart raced, as much at the idea of him wanting her so much as the passion that his kiss incited.

Slowly, gently, he lowered her to the blanket. The soft fluffy fabric brushed erotically against her back, a vivid contrast to the hard strength of his body brushing against the front of her.

Making quick work of her camisole and panties, he slid down her body, the rough hair on his leg scraping erotically over the softer flesh of her inner thighs. His mouth took her nipple, sucking and nipping in delicious torment.

His hand skimmed her hips and he shifted so he could curve his fingers deep inside her, tweaking and teasing her wet sex.

His fingers swirled, his mouth sucked. Her mind spun. She couldn't think. It was all too incredible, too wild.

He rubbed his thumb against her sweet spot, making her moan. Stars exploded behind her eyes as a tiny climax ripped through her body.

Larissa shifted, lifting her hips higher, silently begging for more.

"You want me?" he asked, obviously wanting her pleas to be a little louder.

"I want you," she gasped as his thumb pressed again, his fingers dancing in and out, in and out. He played her like he was a master and she was a finely tuned instrument crafted just for his pleasure.

She clenched her thighs, trying to hold his hand still. He wouldn't let her. Her body bucked against his fingers as another orgasm flashed through her.

Jason gently coaxed her back down to earth with soft fingers and tiny kisses. Her head thrown back, eyes closed as the pleasure still shimmered through her body, she felt him move away. Heard the rip of a foil wrapper. Anticipation tightened, her thighs quivered.

She shifted, opening heavy eyes to watch Jason position himself between her legs. She bent her knees, offering herself in silent supplication.

He plunged. She gasped, quaking at the sudden impact. Pleasure screamed through Larissa's body. She arched her back, trying to take him in deeper.

"More," she gasped, trying to breathe as the power of her climax teased and tormented her, just out of reach. "I need more."

Jason shifted lower, his hands slipping under her knees to lift her legs over his shoulders. Larissa's eyes flew open. He shifted higher, lifting the small of her back off the floor. She whimpered at the change in pressure, feeling like he was filling her like never before. Pounding deeper, harder. His face was in shadows as he gripped her thighs, but she knew he was staring down at her. At them.

The idea of it, of him watching their bodies slide together, sent her over the edge. Passion coiled tight in her belly, then released as a huge orgasm washed over her. Larissa's head tilted back and she lifted her body onto her shoulder blades to meet Jason's thrusts.

She whimpered, stars flashing behind her closed eyes as one orgasm after another pounded through her. Her body exploded in delight, her thighs clenching tight as if she could wring every drop of pleasure from him.

Make every drop last.

Because it was the last. This was too good. Too delicious. Even as her body gloried in the incredible feelings, her heart wept at the reality. Desperation added a sharp bite, an edge of pain that only intensified her passion.

If this was it, she'd take as much as she could.

JASON DROVE INTO LARISSA'S BODY, plunging deep and hard.

He jerked, growling so low in his throat, Larissa swore she felt rather than heard him. Needing to watch his pleasure, she pried her eyes open to stare at his taut face. He stared back. His blue eyes glittered, his breath came in pants.

He was so close.

Wanting to push him over the edge, needing to know she had that much power, she scraped her fingernails up her belly to cup her own breasts. He jerked.

She swirled her index fingers around her areolas. He lost rhythm and gasped.

She tweaked her nipples between her thumbs and forefingers. Zinging shots of electric delight zipped through his body, sending him spiraling out of control.

Jason threw back his head and exploded.

He was dimly aware that his climax had sent Larissa over the edge of pleasure once more. This time she gave a high whimper that ended on a cry as he shifted so fast she didn't know he'd moved until his mouth nipped at her inner thigh.

She screamed. Her body convulsed. Her breath came in pants as she came in waves.

He loved it. Loved her.

Breathing hard, Jason tried to stop his head from spinning out of control as the aftershocks of his orgasm pounded through him like a four-point-five earthquake.

Holy shit. He tossed back his head, shaking his sweat-dampened hair off his face with a shudder of pleasure. Had it always been this good? Why the hell had he ever left her bed? His brain was severely lacking blood, so he couldn't remember a thing. But whatever the reason, he'd obviously been an idiot.

And he had no idea how to fix things. Especially now that Larissa only wanted him for his body.

LARISSA COULD BARELY BREATHE. Passionate aftershocks still quaked through her. She was pretty sure time had passed since Jason had blown her mind. Five minutes, ten, four days. Something like that.

She gave an exhausted sigh. Like it was some kind of

signal, he groaned, then moved off of her, sliding behind her as she curled onto her side.

After shifting to take care of the condom, Jason cuddled her close, her back tight against his front, his arms crossed over her stomach. He nuzzled her hair off the back of her neck to scatter soft kisses across her shoulder.

"You really are the romance authority," he said, a hint of laughter in his words.

"There's more to romance than good sex," she said, exhaustion pulling the automatic response from her. If his arms hadn't been holding hers in place, she'd have slapped her hand over her mouth. This wasn't time to climb on her soapbox. Especially since any romance lecture she'd offer would be hypocritical.

"But as good as the sex is, the romance adds a sweet layer to it, right? Kind of like we are hot together regardless, incredibly hot. But adding a little chocolate? Baby, that layer sent us into the stratosphere." He laughed and pressed another kiss over the back of her neck. "Only you could make sexy that sweet. Only you keep me awake at night, desperate for just one more taste."

Larissa's heart melted a little. She didn't know what to do, what to think.

"You know romance better than you give yourself credit for," she murmured softly. Better, actually, than she'd ever given him credit for. It had been easier to perch on her high horse and judge Jason than to shift her own perceptions. Or to admit that maybe it wasn't that they were lacking romance in their relationship, but that the romance she wanted just didn't exist.

That he made her remember all of his good points wasn't just the problem. It was that he made her doubt her own beliefs about romance. He could act so romantic. But the reality was, what they had between them was the epitome of gratuitous sex.

Maybe this sex thing had been a mistake. Because now she wanted things all over again. Things she knew she couldn't have unless she was willing to settle.

Again.

With a sweep of her lashes to hide the distress in her eyes, Larissa focused on gliding her hand over the tempting hardness of his bicep where it crossed over her chest, willing to sacrifice herself to a night of incredible, mind-blowing and meaningless sex to distract herself from that painful little truth.

Because facing it meant questioning her entire belief system.

And she wasn't willing to consider that for someone who wouldn't stick around.

Since Chloe wasn't there, Larissa would never have to admit to being a straight up liar. Instead, she promised herself that since tonight was her own final fantasy, she could do whatever she wanted.

And she wanted to do Jason. Again and again and again.

Rolling over to face him, Larissa scraped her teeth over his nipple. He groaned and his fingers tightened on her butt, pulled her tighter against him.

"Is there more chocolate?" he asked, his breath hot and moist against her throat as he lifted her over his body.

"Enough," she said, gasping as he took her nipple into his mouth. He teased and tormented. Larissa had thought she was satisfied. No, she knew she had been satisfied.

But a whole new need exploded inside her. One that demanded she have him. As much of him, as fast as possible.

As they twined together, their passion climbed higher, flamed hotter.

And the power of their coming together made it easy for her to ignore the tears soaking into her hair.

# *11*

THE AIR WAS HOT AND WET, almost dripping with humidity. Jason's body felt like liquid, he was so relaxed. Curled around Larissa, he sighed and let the pleasure wash over him. It wasn't like he didn't have a whole slew of incredible memories of their times together. Hell, he hauled the memories out every once in awhile just to torment himself.

But this time? It'd been intense. It'd been wild. It'd been like Larissa had tossed aside her inhibitions to kick things up a few—or few dozen—degrees.

He did a quick inventory, trying to assess how long it'd be before all his parts were ready to give it another go.

Then his stomach growled.

Larissa giggled.

"I thought you were asleep," he murmured, brushing a kiss over her hair.

"It's too hot and sticky to sleep," she said with a sigh, turning in his arms. Her body slid damply against his, proving her point.

And turning him on.

Again.

Yep, his parts were definitely considering coming out to

play. Maybe he should get an image of the Energizer bunny tattooed on his ass.

"What'd you have in mind if you're not interested in sleep?" he asked, his hand tracing a swirling pattern on the slick skin of her hip. He was tempted to slide his fingers down and see what else was slick and wet, but before he could decide if his body would do justice to his thoughts, his stomach growled again.

"Maybe you should have eaten that sandwich earlier instead of taking off like that," she teased with a laugh. "Where'd you go, anyway?"

"The janitor's closet," he joked. Actually he'd returned to the lunch room to give them both some space.

It wasn't the aftertaste of that nasty sandwich that made Jason's stomach turn, but a flashback of their dinnertime discussion. His having to admit his father's deficiencies, Larissa shooting his proposition down, the realization of just how bad he'd hurt her.

Definitely unappetizing at the time, and even worse in re-runs. He'd rather lick the chocolate jar than try that again.

"You don't really think you're like your father, do you?" Larissa asked quietly, not meeting his eyes but instead staring at her fingers as they traced a damp pattern on his chest.

"It doesn't matter," he dismissed quickly, wondering if she'd read his mind. "We're here, naked and have at least a dozen condoms left. Why waste time talking about my family?"

"Well, you are the one who brought it up earlier," she added sweetly. So sweetly that he knew she wasn't going to just let the topic go.

Jason stiffened. At least his spine did. Not anything interesting unfortunately. Steeling himself against a discussion he didn't want but could see Larissa leading up to, he tried to think of a distraction.

The lack of stiffness in his happy parts didn't bode well for his favorite method of changing the subject.

"I'm just saying," she continued, her fingers tracing lower and lower. He tried to focus on the soft caress. "You're obviously pissed off at your dad. And with good reason. But have you talked to him? I mean, you two were so close, Jason. I hate to think of you losing a relationship that means so much to you."

"Maybe," Jason muttered. He didn't know what to say—he'd thought the same thing.

"To tell you the truth…" Her voice dropped. So did her hand. He figured he'd focus on the hand. "Your parents intimidated me. A lot, really. I mean, they were totally on the same page. They had the same goals in life and the same interests. But I sort of wondered, didn't your mom ever have other dreams? Other things she wanted in life?"

Sure. His mom had talked a lot, especially as they got older, about settling down for longer periods of time. She'd wanted to plant a garden. To see movies and go out to dinner. But that hadn't been in his dad's plan.

Too bad she'd had to have a stroke to get them. Jason dismissed the thought as stupid, but a part of him wondered if maybe she hadn't been a little relieved to finally have an acceptable excuse to not follow his father on yet another dig.

"I guess it's okay to tell you now, I worried that you'd expect the same from me. That absolute commitment…" Her words trailed off. Jason didn't need to see her face to figure out what she was probably thinking. Maybe he had. And maybe she was right. Hadn't he thought that if she'd just come with him on his travels, she wouldn't have had time to stay home and date other guys? Stupid thought, yes. But he'd had it all the same.

"Nope," he said. Then, not sure why but unable to keep the words quiet, he added, "I mean, I really did enjoy having you along. It was always cool showing you the places I loved, sharing my excitement. But I never expected you to give up your own plans, your own dreams, for mine."

He just wished they could have meshed their dreams together a little better. With his arms wrapped tight around the only woman he'd ever loved, Jason stared off into the dark. Peter was like their dad that way. He expected total devotion. He insisted on bringing Meghan on trips. As many as possible. He always used to warn Jason that he and Larissa were doomed because she wasn't into adventure. Sure, she'd liked the more romantic treks, the ones with a night or two in an exotic hotel or a hut on the beach. According to Peter, once in awhile wasn't good enough. It was all or nothing for the Cantrell men.

Since their dad had seemed to be the same way—although Jason hadn't ever actually asked him—he'd assumed Peter's assessment of the Cantrell men's code was right.

Which was probably why Jason had ended up with nothing.

He nuzzled Larissa's hair with a sigh. Even knowing those things, he couldn't imagine doing it any differently. Larissa deserved her own, incredible life. Proof positive was how she'd built such a great name for herself as a romance expert. Could she have, would she have, done that if they'd been together? Or would he have stifled her instead?

"I guess it doesn't matter in the long run," he muttered, thinking more of his own relationship than his parents'.

"Sure it does. I mean, they made it for a long time, didn't they?" she mused. "That says a lot. They must have had a lot of passion between them."

"What?" he yelped, both grossed out and grateful for the distraction.

"Not the naked kind," she laughed. "You know, more like friendship. Caring and excitement. That kind of thing."

"They were, you know, parents. It wasn't like I was watching their relationship or anything."

Or seeing them as people in their own right, he realized with a frown.

"Were there any hints of a problem before your mom had her stroke?" she asked, finally looking up to meet his eyes. Unfortunately her fingers stopped their sweet distraction, so he had to focus on her.

"I don't know," he said, shrugging one shoulder. "Is it getting stuffy in here? Maybe we should move into the mall. It's a bigger space, more circulation."

"Right, walk out there," she said with a laugh. "No way. What if the electricity comes back on, including the security cameras?"

Jason imagined a bunch of security geeks watching the video of him and Larissa getting wild with the chocolate and decided the first thing he'd do when someone let them out of here would be to destroy those tapes. Before Conner saw them, of course.

"Aren't there cameras in the stores?" Despite his anger at the idea of their private moments being recorded, he'd gladly dance naked for one as a thank you for the subject change.

"No. In-store security is the store's responsibility. Didn't Conner tell you that?"

"I didn't talk to Conner, I talked to Daniel. And to tell you the truth, I didn't listen to half the crap he said. I knew the space was what I wanted. I figure I'd leave the details to Peter."

She hummed a little low in her throat. Like she had something to say about that, but in the interest of keeping the naked peace, she was refraining.

Grateful, Jason brushed a kiss over her bare shoulder and curled her tighter in his arms.

"So do you see your mom often now that she's in a home?" Larissa asked, stubbornly returning to her torment…that was, the topic. She was like one of those little dogs. All cute and fluffy looking, but stubborn as hell when she got her tiny little teeth into something. And too sweet to kick out of his way.

"Often enough," he finally admitted. He hated it, though. It was hard enough seeing his mom as a single person instead of part of a parental unit. It was harder still seeing how broken she'd become. "I drop in. You know, when I'm home and stuff."

Why couldn't Larissa feel how uncomfortable he was? Or maybe she did and she was ignoring it. Was this one of those stupid *for his own good* discussions? The last one of those they'd had ended with the word goodbye.

"Is she excited about Peter's upcoming wedding?"

Why were they talking about his family? Tension curled so tight in his body, his toes ached. He couldn't deal with this. Why couldn't Larissa just stick with pillow talk or compare him to her other sexual conquests? Why did it always have to come around to serious shit that made him want to run screaming from the room?

"Mom's not too focused these days, but it really doesn't matter," he dismissed, wishing he wasn't lying.

"How can it not matter?" she asked. From her puzzled look and the innocent tone, he knew she was seriously confused. Not trying to scrape her fingernails over the chalkboard of his soul.

"It just doesn't, okay." Jason sat up, careful to make it look casual and not like he was trying to jump away.

"Okay," she said slowly. He'd used that same tone once when he'd woke up on safari to find a lion prowling his camp. He knew what that tone meant.

He wanted to get in her face and make her acknowledge that he wasn't bullshitting with her excuses. That he wasn't an emotional commitment-phobic mess with parental issues.

That if anyone would know what mattered—in his past, his present and his damned future—it'd be him, wouldn't it? Yes, dammit, it would.

But that might come off as a *little* defensive.

"I need food," he declared instead, glancing at his watch. "It's almost midnight. Definitely time for a snack."

He didn't even try to lie to himself that he wasn't running away. From his thoughts. From the answers. And yes, maybe he wanted to get away from Larissa, too.

Things had been a lot better when they'd been having sex.

He got to his feet so fast, she almost tumbled off the blanket. With a sheepish apology, he reached out a hand to help her into a sitting position.

"Did you want anything?" he offered, a gentleman to the last, even while running like a pansy girl.

"Maybe some water from the fridge. It might still be cool in there, don't you think?"

Heading out of the store, he gave a noncommittal shrug, not wanting to have to make a decision right now, even on something as simple as his opinion.

"Aren't you going to put on your pants?" she asked. Her look said she knew exactly what he was doing, but she laughed it off. Obviously she didn't want to fight naked any more than he did.

His shoulders itched uncomfortably at the idea of someone—anyone—knowing him that well. It was definitely time to take a break.

Jason glanced at his crumpled jeans in the corner. Just the thought of putting thick denim on in this heat made him cringe. Then he looked down at his body, still sporting splotches of chocolate and wrinkled his nose. "I think I'll hit the bathroom to wash up instead."

She pointed questioningly to his boxers, hanging like a banner off one of the light fixtures.

"Why bother?" he decided as he bent over to give her a kiss before heading out into the mall. "I'm just going to get naked and have my way with you again as soon as I get back."

"There's a bathroom right here," she said, gesturing with one hand toward the back of the store.

Jason felt like there was a rope tightening around his neck. Swallowing past the constriction, he shook his head.

"Nah, there's a bigger one out here. More room to, um, de-chocolate myself and stuff."

"Then don't you at least need a candle?" she called after him as he hurried out.

"Nah, I know where all my stuff is."

Now to get it all put back where it belonged. Hidden away, behind firm emotional barriers. The same place any other well-adjusted man would put it.

HER ARMS WRAPPED AROUND her bent legs, Larissa laid her cheek on her knees and watched Jason's very fine, very naked butt leave.

She didn't know why she was wasting her time wishing he'd open up and actually talk to her. This night wasn't about rekindling their romance. It was simply the consequences of being trapped together and really, really horny.

That was all. She just had to keep those facts in mind and she'd be fine.

Straightening and hooking her elbow to the outside of the opposite knee, Larissa stretched until her back cracked. Then she switched in the other direction. She arched her neck one way, then the other, then back to release tension she hadn't realized she was holding.

"You'd think hot sex and multiple orgasms would have loosened me up," she muttered to herself. And maybe they would have, if it hadn't been for that undertone of angst making her so edgy.

Larissa straightened her legs, arched her toes and stretched her body flat until her fingers gripped her ankles.

"Good thing we're not a couple," she told her knees.

And it was. She was glad she didn't have to do this emotional dance any longer. They weren't a couple, so she didn't need to fixate over what she said and if he was pissed because she'd said it.

No longer would she freak out after attempting to get Jason to emotionally open up. To admit that there was more to him—to them—than surface jokes and great sex.

So she was glad that she wasn't dealing with all of that.

"Nope, all I'm doing is enjoying some great sex to pass the time," she said to the room at large, wondering if her words could really be considered lies if nobody was there to hear and she personally knew she was spouting bullshit. Kinda like the tree in the woods enigma.

Trying to distract herself from the pending depression she felt looming around her like an extra layer of sticky-hot humidity, Larissa imagined Jason's trek through the mall.

Talk about out of his element. He was in a mall instead of some remote jungle.

And, of course, there was the naked thing.

Focusing on the idea of Jason, naked, was the best distraction ever.

He was waltzing naked in front of the likes of Tiffany, MAC and the finest French undies known to women. She giggled at the image, then lay back on the marble floor and tried to soak up some of the coolness of the stone. Eyes closed, she imagined his naked journey and wondered, could she be that comfortable in her nudity?

Not likely, she snorted. She doubted she could step into those stores in anything less than her best dress and most expensive shoes.

She remembered the last time she'd tried to shop in La Perla. The salesman had been so snooty, she'd ended up leaving without buying a thing. Then, out of pure defiance, she'd headed straight to Victoria's Secret and loaded up on panties.

She sure hoped that sales guy didn't end up working at this location. She could just imagine him staring down his nose at her store while he fondled a mannequin's garter belt. He'd definitely consider her offerings too pedestrian to be within gawking distance of his lacy merchandise.

Her grin faded. She glanced at her briefcase, with its carefully detailed business plan. Her eyes shifted to the box of merchandise. Cute stuff. Fun stuff. Pure romance, both sweet and sexy.

It'd work in the bookstore. She could imagine the items scattered around the Victorian, how she'd display them in the rooms. Those kits Chloe made would be perfect in the kitchen with a little sign that suggested the customers cook up a little fun.

She'd repurpose one of the small, cramped parlors with a plush chair and wide-screen television. Maybe a pair of fluffy bunny slippers and a luxurious blanket. She rubbed her fingers over the one currently providing a cushion between her butt and the hard marble. She'd fill the shelves with the romance DVDs she'd sell.

Larissa shook her head, blinking fast to erase the image from her mind.

That was yesterday's dream. A dream that depended on her convincing people to stick around, on her ability to lure customers back to the store time and time again. The only way to keep an independent bookstore in business, let alone a specialty store like she'd want, was customer loyalty. And Larissa had learned the hard way that loyalty in the long term was a myth.

That was why this deal was so perfect. Here, in a hotel, she didn't need to worry about returning customers, since the nature of the location meant the people always changed. Here, she could create an image, expand her role as the romance expert, and nobody would be around long enough to discover it was all a sham.

And she was going to make it work, even if she had to march her department-store-dress-wearing-self into La Perla and face down the snobbiest of the snobs.

She wished Jason would hurry back and distract her from these horrible, soul-baring thoughts. This was why sleep was so important. Not for health reasons, but because these intense, heart-wrenching thoughts always surfaced at two in the morning.

Shoving her damp, humidity frizzed hair off her shoulder, she had to admit, it was so sticky and uncomfortable in here, she wouldn't have been able to sleep anyway. Which meant Jason should be here to distract her, dammit.

Leave it to Jason to go missing when she needed him. Larissa got to her feet and, feeling really naked, looked around for something to wear. She started to perspire at just the thought of wrapping that blanket around herself again. Just as she was wishing the rain would cut through the humidity, or that the windows were breakable, she spied Jason's shirt.

That'd work. She'd just hooked a couple of the buttons when she heard a noise.

Her heart raced.

Ax murderer?

"You'll never guess what I found," Jason said as he came through the entryway.

She sighed a little, her body going into a full-on meltdown at the way the candlelight flickered temptingly over his body. Her eyes slid down the wide expanse of golden shoulders, muscled and glistening. His arms, the same arms she'd gripped so tightly as he drove her over the edge of screaming passion, were curved around…something. She didn't care what. She was just irritated that whatever he held obscured her view of the happy trail aimed down his washboard abs.

Her eyes dropped to the main event.

Even at rest, it made for an impressive show.

Larissa ran her tongue over her lower lip, determined to get another taste. Which meant she had to keep those pesky little observances and personal comments to herself.

Screw romantic connections. She wanted good sex.

"Larissa?"

"Huh?"

"You okay?"

She dragged her eyes back up his body to meet his questioning gaze. He looked so sweet. His hair fell across his forehead, giving him a sexy little bad boy look. She couldn't see the expression in his eyes, but his half-smile was teasing. His stance just a little cocky.

Why was he everything she wanted in a man? And why was most of it locked up so tight inside him that he had no trouble denying it. Even to himself.

She swallowed, hard. Sex, she chanted silently. Remember the sex.

"Yes. Of course. I'm fine."

He gave her a long look, like he was trying to see inside her head and figure out why she was lying. That he knew she was lying was a given.

"Did you want to hear what I found?"

"Sure." Her fingers wrapped around the open plackets of his shirt, tugging them closed. She suddenly felt both overdressed and much too vulnerable.

"What if I told you I found a way out?"

Well, that yanked her right out of Fantasyland. Were they done with the sex? Had she wasted half their sex time trying to get him to admit he had a heart? Larissa's lower lip protruded.

"Really? You found a way out?"

"No," he said with a laugh. "But I did think that'd be your first response. You know, given how you kept going on earlier about getting out of here."

"Sure. Because now that we've gotten naked together, I was hoping you'd hurry up and find that secret way out." Larissa's return smile was a little stiff. So was her middle finger, but she kept that hidden in the fabric of his shirt.

He stopped laughing, his smile dimming a little. "Me, too. But only because I'd rather finish our naked times in a bed than on that floor. But I'm willing to pull the gentleman card and offer to take the bottom for the next few rounds."

Larissa gave him the laugh he wanted. And she didn't point out that their naked times were restricted to this night, this place and this once. He knew that already. But like so much else that Jason knew, he'd rather pretend it wasn't there.

"So what did you find if not a secret passage out of here?" she asked lightly.

"The answer to all your fantasies."

"Johnny Depp is here?"

Jason kept his eye roll small, instead raising his hand to shake the contents a little. Larissa squinted, trying to figure out what he had. It was hard to focus, though, since his shaking sent things swaying.

"It's a bowl?"

"And…?"

"It's a bowl of something that's making a lot of noise?"

He walked slowly forward, his steps reminding her of a stalking animal. A tiny skittering of nerves danced up Larissa's spine. With his eyes on her, she felt frozen in place. Her breasts rose and fell quickly beneath the soft denim shirt. He stopped inches away and, his gaze still locked on hers, lowered the bowl. It was still too high for her to see what was in it, though. Not that it mattered. She couldn't tear her gaze away from his hypnotic blue eyes.

His fingers traced just inside the unbuttoned edges of her—or really, his—shirt, his knuckle skimming her flesh and making her shiver as he left a heated trail. She pressed her thighs together, desire coiling tight between her legs at his touch.

His other hand slipped around behind her. She barely noticed as he skimmed the back of his hand under the shirt.

Then he pressed the icy cold bowl to her back.

Larissa jumped, gasping out a tiny scream.

"I found ice," he said, laughing as he showed her the bowl. "It's melting fast, but there were a few trays in the break room freezer."

"Oh," she breathed, wrapping both hands around the metal container and closing her eyes at the wonderful chill that poured through her palms. "So nice."

"You wanted cool water, I figured this might work."

"Did you bring a glass?" she asked, looking around to see if she'd missed it. Not seeing one, she shrugged and lifted the bowl to her lips, sipping the ice cold water. "Mmm."

She took a deeper drink. Big mistake. The large bowl wasn't made to drink from, so the water slopped over the sides. His eyes narrowed. Rivulets streamed down her chin and over her throat.

Jason gave a low groan.

Despite the ice, Larissa's body started to burn.

He took the bowl from her and, his eyes locked on hers, took a drink. He barely swallowed though. Brow furrowed, she watched him set the bowl on the counter, then he skimmed his hands under the shirt, up her torso and cupped her breasts. His fingers squeezed gently. Larissa's head fell back and she took a deep breath so the fabric of the shirt separated. He released one breast to flick open the few buttons, then bent down and wrapped his lips around her hardening nipple.

"Omigosh," she breathed, shocked at the intensity of the feelings pouring through her. His mouth was hot. The ice was cold. The contrasts were incredible.

Icy water dripped down her breast, over her stomach. He grabbed another ice cube and slid it along her hip. She listened, surprised it didn't sizzle on her hot body.

Then he pressed his palm against the wet heat of her mound. The ice made her thighs clench automatically. Her gasp ricocheted off the walls. After a quick nip of his teeth on her tight nipple, he kissed the underside of her breast, then skimmed down her torso, open mouthed, until he was kneeling in front of her. Her legs wobbled. He wrapped one arm around her hips to help support her as he nudged her thighs apart.

He stared into her eyes, a dark promise of delight in the

blue depths of his as he popped the ice cube into his mouth. Holding her gaze until the last second, he licked his freezing tongue over her already swollen and well-pleasured sex. The chill was incredible. Invigorating and seductive.

Then his fingers slipped inside her. First one, swirling and plunging. Then two. He sucked harder. Her body shook. He sent her up so fast, so hard, she couldn't think straight. All she could do was dig her fingers into his shoulders and hold on for the ride.

Her climax was wild and intense. Her body rocked against his mouth. She shivered at the power he had over her, but couldn't find it in her to care. If the man could play that kind of magic on her body, he was welcome to do it anytime.

After a few seconds, she decided turnabout was only fair. When she knew her knees would support her, she stepped away.

And reached for the bowl.

"Whatchya doin'?" he asked in a raspy tone.

"Paying you back," she promised just before she slipped a couple pieces of melting ice into her mouth and knelt in front of him.

As far as distractions went, an iced-down blow job was top of the list for keeping her focus off her breaking heart.

## 12

WAKING SLOWLY AND THROWING OFF the groggy fog of a couple hours sleep, Larissa stretched her arms overhead, trying to work a few of the kinks out of her sore body. Who knew an ice cube blow job could be that exhausting. She gave a luxuriant smile, feminine power pouring through her and bringing almost as much pleasure as her earlier orgasms.

Okay, maybe not nearly as much. But a lot of pleasure. She grinned, loving this feeling. Missing how good it was to be not just a woman, but a sexual being.

She glanced around, looking for the man to thank for the experience. Nada. Maybe he was in the bathroom?

She stood, wincing as her thighs screamed. Wow, it'd been a long time since her body had been a sexual being. Having really, *really* good sex used muscles she'd forgotten she had. She took a couple mincing steps, groaning a little. She looked around, glad Jason wasn't here to witness her lack of grace.

And speaking of really, really good sex…and Jason— where was he?

Her pleasure fading a little, she glanced at the open bath-room door and didn't see any candlelight. She frowned, noting that his jeans and shirt were still crumpled on the ground. But his boxers weren't flying from the sconce any longer.

Which meant he was at least semi-dressed. Wherever he was.

Apparently she was the only one who was having trouble walking after their sexy times.

As usual.

Larissa bent over, grabbing Jason's shirt off the floor and shrugging it on. She shoved the buttons through the holes, her teeth clenched.

His scent wrapped around her as warmly as the fabric. She fingered the cuffs, then shoved them up her arms as she stomped toward the front of the store to glare out into the mall.

Seriously. It was the middle of the night. Where the hell was he? Why couldn't he stick around for just a little while? Hadn't the night been incredible for him, too? Hadn't he groaned and moaned and had a wild old time? Hadn't it been worth sleeping in each other's arms for at least a few hours? She squinted at her watch, noting it was half past three in the morning. She wondered how many minutes he'd held out after she'd dropped into sleep before heading off. Five? Maybe ten?

Shoulders hunched, she stared down one side of the mall, then the other. She twisted her fingers together. She could go look for him. But that would make her look desperate, wouldn't it? Or was it more pathetic to be found waiting here for him like a lovesick girl, her happiness hinging on his return.

Larissa tilted her head back, staring at the ceiling and blinking fast to clear the tears from her eyes. How did she end up here again? Had she learned nothing in the last few years? Was she so pathetic that she couldn't resist Jason's magic dick? Or was this a sad little romantic fairy tale she kept falling into, thinking that somehow, some way, they had a future. Together.

Larissa crossed her arms over her chest, pacing back and forth in the doorway.

This was supposed to have been one last fling. A chance to do all those naughty things she'd missed out on the last time with Jason, but to do them the smart way. Knowing it was just sex, she would not only have her fun, but finally put to rest her internal struggle with that one question… Could she settle for a relationship that was all about sex, knowing there was no emotion involved?

Larissa's pacing had brought her to the back of the store, to their love nest. The mohair blanket was balled into a soft bundle, Jason's clothes were strewn against the wall and an empty chocolate jar tilted on its side like a drunken soldier.

All evidence of decadent, intensely satisfying sex.

The only thing missing, as usual, was Jason himself.

Which said it all.

Larissa shook her head, the stomping sound of her bare feet against the marble taking her pacing to an angrier level. She really was pathetic. She couldn't believe she'd actually believed, somewhere deep in the hidden recesses of her heart, that he'd take one look at her again and fall in love.

Or that if they gave in to their passion, he'd give up wanting to do all that traveling and wish he could build a life with her.

Larissa clenched her fists and growled. Because believing all that crap had worked so well for her the first time.

She stopped mid-pace to stare at the counter where Jason had stripped her bare the first time last night. A tear trickled down her cheek. Talk about a sucky time to face reality. At least last time, she'd had Conner there to distract her. She should be grateful he was nearby for this round, too.

"Hey, looking for me?"

Larissa spun to face Jason, who stood there looking like sexy temptation, his boxers thankfully covering those tempting magic parts. He had a large, Maglite-type flashlight in one hand and a few bottles of water in his other.

"No," she told him in a distant tone as she surreptitiously wiped her cheek and wished, not for the first time, that he'd made it easier and just stayed away. "I was just getting a feel for the floor footage. It made sense to get to know the area since I'll be working here."

His smile downgraded. "What's wrong?"

"Why would anything be wrong?"

"Number one, you sound irritated. Number two, you're talking all formal again. And three, you haven't come over here to kiss me or slide your hand down my boxers. So something's obviously bothering you."

Larissa opened her mouth, wanting to point out that there was more between them than just sex. Then she closed it. Because, truthfully, there wasn't.

"Nope," she replied with a friendly, totally fake, smile. "Nothing's wrong. Like I said, I was doing a little planning. Getting comfortable in the space, you know?"

"Comfortable?" Responding to her anger by dumping his armload of stuff on the counter, he turned to face her with his arms clamped over his deliciously bare chest. "Yeah. You seem really relaxed and mellow here."

"I'm focusing on business. You know how that goes, don't you? Of course you do," she continued, finally losing her grip on that emotional control. "You know all about how important it is to put work first. You're the king of business first, aren't you?"

"Why would you be thinking business after the way

we've spent the last few hours?" He narrowed his eyes, getting that same wigged-out look on his face that he'd had earlier, before he'd gone on his ice run. "Or was it only some twisted way of trying to talk me out of competing for the storefront here?"

Larissa's lingering tears disappeared.

He actually thought that after everything that had happened between them, she'd be standing here trying to figure out how to screw him over? Her? Screw *him* over?

A voice in the back of her head pointed out that if she'd thought she could influence him, she'd probably have tried. Not on her knees perhaps, but still...

Yet more proof that Jason wasn't the man for her. She grabbed onto that realization, and the stirring anger, and held on tight. She needed to emotionally step back and, as usual, he'd just given her the opening.

"So where were you off to?" she asked. "Still trying to find a way out?"

"Just exploring."

"What's left to explore? I'd have thought you'd seen it all by now."

"Sometimes it's fun to check it out again. See if you missed anything the first time."

She rolled her eyes.

"I doubt you missed anything. There's this small mall area, a lunchroom, janitor's closet and storeroom. What the hell else is there to see?" she asked, ignoring the double entendre. "That was the third time you disappeared since we've been here."

"Not that you were counting or anything?"

Glad the darkness hid her blush, Larissa just shrugged. "Hey, at least I can always count on you leaving."

"Where the hell was I going to go?" he snapped, starting to sound impatient. "You said it yourself. We're trapped."

"Your own version of hell," she quipped.

"You keep saying things like that. What's it supposed to mean?" He punctuated the question with a fist in the air, like he was so frustrated that he had to hit something.

She rolled her eyes. "You've said it yourself. You can't stand to stay in one place."

"Adventures are pretty boring if they are done in one place, don't you think?"

"Life should be more than an adventure, shouldn't it?"

He gave her a penetrating look and shook his head. "What's the deal? You're taking my business so personally. Like it's all about you or something."

"Of course it's not about me," she defended. Then, before she knew it, the words escaped, "But if you really cared, you'd have given enough of a damn to actually consider me."

Jason shook his head, making her feel even more pathetic. He was like an emotional magnifying glass, damn him. She pressed her hand to her stomach, suddenly wanting to throw up.

"I don't get it, Larissa. You've got this insane inferiority complex. You're smart. You're sexy. You're sweet and gorgeous and talented. But when you say shit like that, it's like you're insecure or something. What's the deal?"

What? Like she was supposed to drag out her bag of neurosis and spread it across the floor for him to poke through? Hardly. Larissa shook her head.

"If I was all that, why did you leave me?" she asked. Horrified, she clamped her lips together and wished the words back. Oh, God. That's not what she'd meant to say. She'd never, ever meant to ask him that. Her pride, and her heart, didn't need the agony.

"What?" She didn't need the sputtering light of the candle to see the shock on his face. His tone was clear enough.

"You left," she said quietly. She wanted to get up and run away instead. But where? She was trapped, both literally and figuratively. "You took my engagement ring and you walked out."

"You went out with Conner," he replied, for the first time sounding hurt instead of cockily irritated. "Then when I got pissed about it, you handed me the ring and told me to leave. What the hell was I supposed to do?"

The heat of her glare combined with the tears wetting her lashes made it feel like there was steam billowing from her eyes. Fury, fear, pain, they all mixed together to tangle her thoughts and make her want to scream.

She didn't know what she'd wanted him to do. To convince her that they could make it? To refuse to let her end things? To freaking fight and prove he loved her enough to want to stick around?

Yeah. She'd wanted all of that. But she'd also wanted him to leave. To take the broken dreams of a perfect romance and constant heartache of failure and go. Because she'd been sure it would be easier to live, to succeed and believe in herself, if she wasn't always waiting for him to realize she wasn't enough for him and leave on his own.

Horrified at the realization, she clamped her lips tight together to keep from crying out.

"That's all in the past," she said quickly, thankful that her voice was only a little choked up. "I'm sorry I brought it up. Let's talk about now, instead."

"Now?" he said suspiciously.

"Sure." She floundered, mentally flailing around trying to find something safe about now. Desperate, she glommed onto what he'd said earlier. "Let's talk about the store and how much better your business would do if you set it up in a different location."

"I knew it," he said. "You do want me up to change my plans, don't you?"

Larissa threw her hands in the air. "Of course you should change your plans. They're crazy. They don't fit your business model, nor this location."

"My plans aren't any crazier than yours. You're trying to fluff up a pussycat and make it into a tiger. Your idea isn't tiger-worthy, Larissa."

She felt like a million needles were stabbing her in the heart.

"What kind of stupid thing is that to say?" she asked, blinking the black spots away.

Jason shook his head, then strode over to grab up his jeans and shove his legs into them. Avoiding her eyes, he yanked the zipper up with such force that Larissa winced, glad she had finished playing with the package, since he probably just damaged it.

"Forget it," he finally said as he snapped his pants.

"No. You meant something with that stupid cat analogy. Maybe you can put it in English so it's clear what you mean," she challenged, shoving her chin out to keep it from trembling.

"Let's not do this, Larissa." He backed away, shaking his head and sounding tired. She ignored his tone, focusing instead on the fact that, as usual, he was running from her.

"Why? Because it might hurt our non-relationship to be honest with each other? Why don't you tell me how you really feel? You know, like you never did when we were together."

Well, that got his attention off his fly.

"Aren't you the one hiding?" he asked, his tone somewhere between taunting and pitying. "Using this as yet another excuse to run away from your dream? You could be living the life you always talked about, but you keep holding out until the perfect time. The perfect scenario. How long is it going to take before you accept that life isn't perfect?"

Her heart pounded so loud, she was surprised it didn't echo through the empty room. Larissa stared, blinking a few times to process his question.

When the answer hit her, she felt like she'd been punched in the gut.

He was right. She looked around the opulent store and all of the doubts that she'd had about fitting in here, and at the mall, crashed over her. Her perfect dream was to take over the bookstore. But she'd set that dream aside for this one.

Why? Because she'd created that dream when she was with Jason. She realized that whenever she thought about the bookstore, her image was of herself, married to Jason. Waiting and nurturing her business while he traveled. Raising their children in that darling location after they'd bought the house next door to live in.

Jason was such an integral part of that future, she'd had to give it up when he was no longer a part of her life.

Larissa swallowed back the pain that lodged in her throat and gave Jason a nonchalant shrug.

"I know life isn't perfect," she said, forcing the words out. "But at least I'm smart enough to know what I'm capable of instead of diving in over my head because I'm too cocky to be realistic."

"Does this circle back to your brilliant assessment of how I should be running my business?"

"You mean ruining your business?"

"How's that unlike what you're doing? You're going to give up a great location where you're already established, all to chase a bit of glitter and gloss?"

"At least I understand the wisdom of making a plan

instead of diving in with both feet and crossing my fingers I don't break my ankles when I hit bottom," she snapped.

"Yep, that's you. The queen of the plan. You're so busy planning, you don't live. You spend so much time dreaming about what could be, you never actually live in the moment," he told her.

"What are you? A self-help guru all of a sudden?" she challenged, her shoulders stiffening defensively. "Live in the moment? Where do you get that crap?"

"From you," he barked.

They both slammed their mouths shut so fast and tight, the sound of teeth snapping echoed in the room.

"You know this isn't right for you. Your idea is cute. It's romantic and fun and clever, yes. But it's not high end. You can try and make it work here," he said, waving his hand around the store. "But it'll never fit in. Not really. Not the way you want it to."

Was he talking about her business? Or their failed relationship? She'd never realized how alike the two things were. Larissa hated him for saying out loud all the things she'd been secretly worrying about.

"I'll fit just fine," she defended weakly. "At least I'll do better than you would. You're talking about putting a travel agency into a mall that caters to the wealthy and pampered. How does that tie in with the theme and message Cartright is trying to put together here?"

The air changed. Humid and tense turned to hot and ugly in the blink of Jason's blue eyes. Larissa gulped, mentally kicking herself.

"Cartright. You mean Conner, don't you?"

Oh shit. He was so pissed. Larissa wished she could hide somewhere, but there was nowhere to go. Between his clenched jaw, his narrowed eyes and the waves of fury emanating off of him, she figured this was a smart time to shift gears. Not to back pedal, but maybe to stop poking him in the eye with a sharp stick.

"It doesn't matter," she forced herself to say with a jerk of her shoulders. "That's the past, right?"

"Right. The past. So I should just forget that while we were engaged, you spent the weekend yachting with another man?"

She was so freaking sick and tired of carrying that unfair blame that she finally snapped, giving a little scream and tugging on her hair. Damn him for not trusting her, even after all this time.

"Another man, and twenty other friends," she said through clenched teeth.

Looking shocked—whether from her scream or her words, she didn't care—Jason frowned, crossing his arms over his still bare, and oh, God help her, still tempting chest.

"You never told me there were other people there," he accused, stepping closer so he towered over her.

"You never asked," she offered back, her tone so saccharine sweet, sugar could have dripped on her toes.

"I shouldn't have had to ask. A simple sentence from you and we wouldn't have had a fight." He glared down at her, his hands now fisted on his hips. "We wouldn't have split up."

Larissa shook her head so fast, her humidity-dampened curls smacked her in the cheeks. "We'd have still spilt up. You didn't trust me. You believed I'd cheat on you. Why should I bother to defend myself if you didn't love me enough to have faith? Faith in me. Faith in us."

FAITH? WHAT THE HELL was Larissa talking about? Jason shook his head, wondering how much long-term damage reading all those romance books had done. She actually thought he was supposed to have faith, even in the face of proof to the contrary? She really did believe in fairy tales.

"That's such bullshit," he replied, fury pounding through his head. He didn't know if he wanted to believe her or wanted her to be lying.

"No," she snapped. "That's such reality. You never cared enough to trust me and you never cared enough to stick around. We had no future."

Yeah, he'd rather she was lying. Lying would mean she'd had faith in him and was just trying to hurt him back. Lying would mean that she'd believed in them. That she'd really loved him.

"You could have come on the trips with me," he added, struggling to pull his thoughts past the anger pounding against his temples. "I asked you plenty of times. It wasn't my fault you had to mind the store or some other crappy excuse."

"You think my reasons for not dropping everything in my life and running off to play Jane of the Jungle with you were crappy excuses?"

Jason shoved his hand through his hair, then gave a whatever shrug. He should have left it alone. So she was irritated. Trying to find out why only led to these dreaded emotional time-sucks, *discussions*.

He hated discussions.

But at least she didn't sound snotty anymore.

He was man enough to admit, he didn't know women well enough to know if that was a good thing or not.

"I think you could have made more changes. A few concessions," he admitted finally, hoping to derail any future discussing. If he could bury his anger, she could skip the discussion. It was only fair. "I mean, if you'd had your way, I'd have done all the changing while you called the shots."

She narrowed eyes that suddenly looked like they could

flame-broil him. "Let me get this straight. In your opinion, we split up over a power play?"

Starting to feel stupid standing there in his underwear, Jason clamped his arms over his chest and nodded. "Yeah, that about fits. It was your way or the highway. And when I wouldn't change, you went out with someone you thought would fit your pre-determined role of the perfect guy."

"Well, it's a good thing you know all the highways and byways, then, isn't it? So you didn't get lost as you ran out the door."

"Ha ha. Why don't you drop the sarcasm and get serious?"

Jason winced, wondering if he were hearing things as the words echoed in the suddenly still room. He wanted the words back even more than he wanted his pants.

"Serious?" She slowly advanced, looking like a vengeful fairy about to curse him. "And you thought it was all about a power play? I tried to talk seriously with you for a year. To work out a way that we could have a future together. That we could grow and build a life. But all you wanted to do was keep going out to play. And you want me to get serious?"

"See, all of that crap sounds boring. It sounds like hell. Who wants a life of growing and building? That's work," he snapped. So much for burying the anger. He shook his head, wondering how so much stuffiness could be packed into such a sexy body. "Life should be fun. An adventure, a good time. Life's about more than dreaming and working, Larissa."

He waited for her defensive response. For her to tell him all the reasons why he was wrong. His shoulders tensed as he prepped for the blow.

But…nothing. She gave him a long look, then just shook her head and turned to walk away.

"Where are you going?" he called, wincing and hoping he hadn't hurt her. God, what was wrong with him? He'd made plenty of mistakes. Who was he to lecture Larissa on how to live life?

"Does it matter?"

"Does this mean we're not going to fight?"

"Why would we?" She stopped and gave him a look over her shoulder. It was one of those casual, barely interested half smile looks. "It's not like it matters, right?"

With that, she headed off into the dark. Jason stood there, his feet rooted on the floor, as he tried to sort through his reactions.

*Shock.* How could she say it didn't matter? He knew it did. It was the core reason for their splitting up, so of course it mattered. But she sounded like she didn't even care.

*Hurt.* Why would she sleep with him if she hadn't cared? Larissa wasn't the purely physical type. She had to feel something to get naked with a guy. Dammit, he'd felt her expectations. He'd heard the silent wishes and hopes and dreams she'd laid at his feet.

*Anger.* Who the hell was she to decide that their relationship wasn't worth fighting for?

Jason let all of those emotions propel him as he stormed down the mall to pace until he regained control. Ten minutes later, he headed back to the store to find her and finish this discussion. But Larissa wasn't there. The candle was down to the bottom of the jar, just a black wick in a pool of scented liquid. Her bag and shoes were right where she'd left them, so he knew she hadn't discovered some secret escape hatch.

He found her at the far end of the mall by the wall of glass and entry doors. She was curled up on one of the benches, her hands cushioning her head as she stared out at the stormy sky.

"So, what's the game?" he asked as he reached her.

She must have heard him coming, because she didn't seem startled. She didn't even turn her head to look at him when she shrugged and answered, "Again, why would I bother with a game? Like I said, it doesn't matter any longer."

"How can you say it doesn't matter?"

This time she did look at him. Her face was set. He could see something in her eyes, but the light was too dim for him to tell if it was hurt, resignation or anger.

"We're not a couple. We're not together. We have no future. So, given all of those reasons, I feel totally justified in saying it just doesn't matter."

"What about last night?" He sounded like a girl but he didn't care.

"What about last night?"

"Didn't that mean anything to you? We spent hours having the best sex either of us have ever had—or are ever likely to have again. We blew each other's minds. It was fucking incredible." His voice was echoing loudly off the walls now, but Jason didn't bother to bring it down. "Are you trying to claim that wasn't good for you?"

"No. You're right," she said, swinging her feet around to the floor so the blanket fell away. He frowned, realizing she was dressed in her camisole and skirt again. Why wasn't she wearing his shirt? "The sex was amazing."

"But?"

"But—" she shrugged "—it was just sex. It wasn't anything more."

"There's more between us than sex," he said, not sure why it mattered that she acknowledge that, but knowing it did.

"No, Jason." She met his eyes, giving him a long, sad

look that made him feel like he'd been kicked in the gut. "There's nothing between us."

He frowned, shoving his hands in his pockets and wishing like crazy for more than the pale shadow of moonlight so he could read her face. Because her voice was blank, and that was killing him.

"There could be," he muttered, not sure what he was going for here, but unwilling to just let it all go. He wanted to talk more. Even though anger was burning a hole in his gut, his regret was even stronger. He'd made his share, more than his share, of mistakes in their relationship. But she'd let him think she'd cheated on him. He wanted, needed, to know why.

For the first time in his life, Jason wanted to sit down and talk things through. To work at it until they'd fixed all their problems. Even if they couldn't have a future together, he still wanted them to be...okay.

"No. You were right. I need life to be a certain way, to live up to my dreams. But we'll never fit that dream. We are just too different. I'm a romantic." He started to protest, but she shook her head and put out a hand to stop his words.

"I'm a romantic dreamer," she repeated quietly, heartbreakingly. "And you're like your father."

The emotional kick to the gut came fast and ugly. Jason blinked away the furious pain, but couldn't think of a response.

"But hey," she said, giving a watery laugh that he knew was supposed to sound cocky instead of miserable. "At least we had a good time saying goodbye, right?"

Good time? That was it?

He felt so...used.

Which was a damn sight better than the miserable feeling of his heart crumbling in his chest.

# _13_

SITTING ON THE FLOOR at the far end of the mall, Jason rested the back of his head against the wall and stared through blurry eyes at the ceiling. Early morning sunshine streamed through the windows and skylights, filling the space with pale pink light.

Larissa's words echoed through his head. Her scent wrapped around him, still lingering on both his skin and the shirt she'd left on the counter like a one hundred percent pure cotton Dear John letter.

What the hell had happened? A day ago, he'd just finished a great trip, negotiated a killer deal on a huge dick-in-a-box and was plane hopping his way home, heart whole and worry free, his only concern snagging his shoe-in spot here in the mall.

And now? Now his head hurt almost as much as his heart. He felt like shit, doubts pounded through his mind like tiny, destructive jackhammers and he no longer gave a rat's ass about the future he'd devoted most of his life to creating.

Without moving his head, he shot a glare down the length of the mall toward Larissa's cozy little nest on the bench. He wanted to blame her. He wanted to say it was all her fault that he was having all these doubts. He'd have been perfectly happy if he'd never seen her again. Well, maybe not happy, but content.

And now?

Now all he wanted was to figure out how to keep her in his life. How to fix things, the right way this time, so they could have a future together.

Jason was finally starting to realize what she used to mean when she'd said there were some dreams worth devoting a lifetime to. That there were things that meant so much, you wanted them to be a part of every single day. Before, he'd always thought his freedom was that dream.

He'd been willing to adjust that freedom—a little—for Larissa. He'd thought about cutting back on his trips. He'd had a few fantasies about maybe moving in with her, spending those weeks he was in town living at her place. Sleeping in her bed.

He'd been such a total ass.

Jason dropped his head into his hands and sighed. He'd blown it. Larissa was right. He was like his father. A jerk who couldn't put anyone's happiness above his own. Except when it came to sex. There, he'd been more than willing to let her go first. First, second and third.

But given Larissa's belief in a happy-ever-after over, what did she call it? Gratuitous sex? Yeah, a few screaming orgasms probably hadn't scored him nearly enough points to balance out the many ways he'd failed her.

But, hey. This was fine. Sure, he'd caused another round of misery and pain. But really, nobody could point any fingers, right? This time they hadn't made any promises.

And last time, he'd been duped.

Jason blinked his sleep-deprived eyes, trying to bring his knees into focus. Frowning, he lifted his head and stared blindly toward the other end of the mall.

Last time, Larissa had duped him. She'd let him think

she'd cheated on him. She'd set him up, watched him take the bait and let him fail. Fists clenched, Jason replayed their conversation, filtering through the guilt and pain and focusing on Larissa's words.

She'd known he had misunderstood the situation. Misunderstood, hell, Conner had straight up told him he and Larissa had been out for a special evening, what else was he supposed to think? But she'd known that not only had nothing happened between her and Conner, but that there was a huge difference between her spending the weekend on a romantic yachting cruise with another man and her going on a boating weekend with a group of friends.

She'd known all of that. But still, she'd expected him to believe that nothing had happened between her and a guy who was her perfect storybook hero. A guy who was always around. Who was rich and successful and could do all that fancy hero stuff that she liked to read about. A guy who, as they all knew, had a secret thing for her.

What else was he supposed to believe when faced with all of that, combined with her silence when he'd asked—okay, maybe accused—her of going out with him? It'd been like the culmination of all of Jason's secret fears. That he wasn't good enough for her, that he wasn't the kind of guy she really wanted to spend her life with. Hell, he'd even wondered if he'd done all that traveling because he was afraid of what he'd find out about himself if he stayed in one place.

Because of her, he'd had a million and one self-doubts. So he'd fought back by traveling more, by proving to them both that he was exciting and fun. And she'd fought back by letting him think she was more interested in someone else than in him.

And he was supposed to have complete faith? What good was faith? Skills and talent and bravery. Those things counted. Faith? Faith was as much a fairy tale as those damned romance novels Larissa read.

Screw faith. She'd lied to him. Maybe not in so many words, but a lie of omission was still a lie.

There. Now it wasn't his fault. Jaw clenched, Jason stared at his fists, balled on the top of his upraised knees. Nope. Not his fault.

Which didn't do a damned thing to make him feel better.

Because it didn't matter whose fault it was. He'd hurt Larissa. Again. And that's why he was hurting. Not over anything she'd done.

God, he was a freaking idiot.

He slowly rose, his aching body protesting as he stretched to his full height and tried to peer down the long mall.

Would she listen if he apologized?

Would it make any difference?

He took three steps, then stopped.

What was he doing? There was no point in trying to charm her into forgiving him if he was just going to wave goodbye and head off on yet another adventure. They were better off letting this thing, whatever it was between them, go. Even if it was ending ugly.

Hey, this way he might be able to put her off his radar once and for all and start looking at other women. Maybe.

Nodding, sure he was making the right decision, Jason was halfway down the mall toward Larissa when he heard a sound.

Buzzing. Electrical buzzing.

The lights flickered dimly in the wall sconces.

Air trickled through the vents. Warm and sluggish at first, then slowly filling the room with cool relief.

"Yes!" Jason did a fist pump in the air and patted his pockets for the keys to the front door. Nothing.

Buttoning his shirt as he went, he strode barefoot into the store to see if the keys Conner had left were anywhere to be seen.

Still nothing.

He'd have to ask Larissa. He grimaced, taking the time to put his socks and shoes on to prepare for the confrontation.

And the pending goodbye.

Slower now, Jason made his way down the mall. Larissa's curls fell around a face soft and beautiful in sleep. Lush lashes curved against her pale cheeks and she had her head resting on her folded hands.

Jason stood there, his hands fisted in his pockets and stared.

How was he supposed to say goodbye?

And how could he not?

LARISSA SIGHED, Jason's spicy scent filling her senses as she breathed deeply the cool air. She snuggled deeper into the blanket and tried to reclaim her sweet dream, the image of her and Jason holding hands filling her mind.

Something kept pulling her out, though.

Slowly, reluctantly, she dragged her eyes open. Jason was right there, his face next to hers with that lock of hair hanging across his forehead to tempt her fingers.

"Hi," she said, sure she was still dreaming. She reached out to sweep the back of her fingers over his scruffy cheek. The prickle of hair brought her crashing back to reality.

This wasn't a dream.

When was she going to accept that fact, dammit?

"Hi back," Jason said quietly.

She slowly blinked the fog out of her eyes, then frowned. Jason's face was too close. She pulled back a little, noting that he'd crouched down in front of her and was staring.

She wet her lips, wishing desperately for a toothbrush.

"What?" she said in a husky tone.

"Do you have the keys to the front door?"

She blinked again, trying to marshal her thoughts into some semblance of clarity. "Keys?"

"The power's on."

He sounded disappointed.

Larissa's frown deepened. She blinked a couple times, trying to see if that regret was echoed on his face. But Jason was too well-versed in the art of the poker face. He just stared back at her with those gorgeous blue eyes.

"The power? We can leave?" she asked.

"I just need the keys."

Larissa sat up, swinging her still blanketed feet to the floor. Jason didn't budge. Despite the cooler air now circulating, heat flashed through her body. Her nipples budded beneath the soft silk of her camisole and her heart beat faster. Even now, as angry as she was at him, he made her crazy with desire.

Her gaze traced his face. Even with lines of exhaustion etched on his tan skin, he was gorgeous. His hair was mussed, a beard shadowing his strong jaw. And his lips. Full and enticing, they were just so close. Close enough to touch. To taste.

She almost whimpered with the need for one more kiss.

"Larissa?"

She blinked, shifting her gaze from his lips to meet his puzzled blue eyes.

"The keys?"

Right. He could finally escape.

Angry at herself, and at him, she tried to shove all those lusty feelings away. Then he held out his hand to help her up, his fingers warm and strong as he offered her support.

And the lusty feelings went all lovey-dovey. Larissa knew better. She knew his romantic gestures weren't enough to overcome all the issues, but dammit, she wanted them to be.

As soon as she was on her feet, she pulled her hand from his and made a show of brushing at the wrinkles on her ruined skirt.

Out of the corner of her eye, she saw him look toward the door and the freedom beyond. That's right, he needed the keys to escape.

"I think I threw them in my briefcase," she said, her words clipped.

"You're angry?" he asked, giving her a hooded look.

"Only with myself."

"Because?"

"Because I never learn," she muttered, turning her back on him under the pretext of folding the blanket. She kept folding until she heard his footsteps depart. She stared through tear-blurred eyes at the tiny, fat square blanket she'd ended up with, and sighed.

By the time Jason was back a couple minutes later, the keys jingling in his hand, she had control of herself again. Her face blank, she watched him put the key in the lock and turn it. She waited for the security bars to rise.

Nothing. She hurried over and opened the panel on the wall next to the door. There were a series of buttons, but she didn't know the code. She felt Jason's warm body behind her, then heard him swear.

"I guess we're still stuck for a while," he said, sounding more resigned than angry.

Larissa turned around, her breath catching when she saw how close he was. Tilting her head up to look into his face, she arched her brow.

"You're crowding me," she told him. Knowing she was

tempting fate, she pressed both palms against his chest to try and push him back. He didn't budge. But oh, baby, his chest felt wonderful. Hard and warm, her fingers tingled as they curled into the soft cotton of his shirt.

"I know," he replied, reaching up to brush her tangled curls off her cheek, then sliding his finger along her jaw. "I can't seem to help myself."

"You're going to have to. We've already established that last night was a mistake."

"Did we?"

She swallowed, having to get past the lump in her throat before she could reply.

"Didn't we?"

"I thought we established that we'd made mistakes in how we'd handled things between us in the past. Not that things between us were a bad thing."

Eyes huge, Larissa studied his face, trying to figure out if he meant that he didn't think it'd been a mistake to open that door between them again. Did this mean he wanted more? That he thought they had a future?

She was afraid to ask—even herself.

Before she could figure out how to extricate herself from this conversation and the probable heartbreak that would go with it, there was a sound at the far end of the mall.

"Well, good morning."

Larissa jumped back from Jason so fast, she banged the back of her head on the wall behind her. Wincing, she rubbed the forming lump as she looked past his shoulder.

"Conner?" she whispered.

Jason's jaw clenched and he closed his eyes as if praying for patience—or mentally cussing up a blue streak. Then he gave a deep sigh and turned around, too.

"Conner," he greeted, stepping forward to shake their friend's hand. "Here to release us?"

"Man, I'm so sorry. You've been here all night, haven't you?" He gave them both a long look, his gaze lingering for a second on Larissa's bare shoulders. She quickly wrapped the blanket around her, grateful she'd put her skirt back on. "I just got a call from security that the motion sensors detected movement and realized what must've happened."

"What's up with the power?" Jason asked.

"The entire eastern seaboard is out. Something about the power grid being overtaxed due to the heat wave. I'm so sorry. If you'd called, I'd have tried to figure out how to get you out."

"No cell," Jason said. Conner nodded. Larissa just stood there. She didn't know what to do. Jason knew there hadn't been anything between her and Conner, so why did he sound so irritated?

"So how are the two of you this morning? An entire night together, I'll bet you patched everything up, right?" he asked, sounding like a little boy asking for confirmation of Santa's visit.

"No," Larissa and Jason said in unison.

Conner gave them both a long, intense frown, then shook his head sadly. If Larissa had ever known her father, she figured that's how he would have shown his disappointment.

"Oh. Well." He gave a long hum, like he was mentally regrouping, then raised his brows. "Well, what do you say we all go out for breakfast? Do some talking. Or I can order in."

He was acting all nervous and weird, like some big business deal was riding on his getting the two of them in agreement.

What in the hell was he up to? Larissa's eyes widened. Was he giving the space to someone else?

"What's going on?" Larissa demanded.

Conner grimaced. Then, seeing the impatient look on

both their faces, he finally admitted, "I'd hoped, given a little time together, the two of you would have worked things out."

"Worked things out?" Jason's voice was low. Calm, even. But Larissa heard the furious undercurrent. She stepped between the two men, knowing she wasn't much of a deterrent but hoping they both cared enough about her to hesitate before mowing each other down.

"What are you talking about?" she insisted. Then she thought back to the look on his face the previous day. Mischievous calculation, with a little bit of glee. Her eyes widened. He hadn't… Had he? "Conner?"

"You locked us in here on purpose?" Jason asked, biting off the words.

"Nope. That was fate stepping in to play her part." He looked around the store, taking in the gutted candle and empty jar on the floor, and grinned. "Looks like she did a good job."

Jason growled.

Larissa pressed her hand to his chest to keep him from moving. She was surprised to feel him take a deep breath and calm down at her touch. Blinking quickly to move past the shock that she might actually have some influence on him, she gave Conner a long, furious look.

"I'm not sure if I've got this right," she said in her calmest, sweetest tone. She hoped it disguised her desire to kick him where it hurt. "You arranged to bring Jason and I back together?"

He nodded.

"The meeting, the presentation, that we just happened to end up here at the same time… They were all part of some elaborate scheme?"

He nodded again.

She gave a low growl and her foot twitched. This time

it was Jason who put his hand on her shoulder, calming *her* down.

"Why?" Jason asked, sounding so mellow they might have been talking about the weather.

"Partially because I felt bad about my part in your breakup," Conner admitted, looking sheepish. "I shouldn't have let you think that something had happened between me and Larissa."

"Correcting any assumptions about our relationship was up to Larissa, not you."

Jason's words made her wince. He was right. Instead of telling him the truth when she should have, she'd used his accusation as an excuse to justify her own doubts. She'd seen his lack of trust as a way to get out before he realized he'd made a mistake.

Larissa pressed her lips together to keep from crying as she realized she was as bad as she'd always accused Jason of being. First chance to escape and she'd taken it. And she'd used Conner in the process. All because she was a chicken who was so afraid to fail at romance that she'd throw away her chance at having a real relationship. A relationship that meant ups and downs, highs and lows. Yes, there would be romance and great sex, but there'd be fights and disappointments, too.

She'd spent so much of her life reading romance novels and sighing enviously when the couple declared their love, then closing the book at the end, that she didn't know what to do—what to expect—after the *I Love You* part.

"Well, whoever it was up to, I felt bad. I mean, you two had a good thing going. You were clearly meant to be together and it sucked that things ended the way they did," Conner explained, now talking a little faster as he stepped out of his comfy CEO role and backslid into acting like a geeky teenager trying to make his buddies happy. "Even if you didn't go forward together, I thought maybe if you could heal the past, you might be able to go forward separately."

Larissa just stared, not knowing what to say. Jason crossed his arms over his chest. She figured they were all better off not knowing what he wanted to say.

"I wanted to try and put things right," Conner muttered.

"You waited all this time to *put things right?*" she asked incredulously.

He nodded.

"Couldn't you have strapped on a diaper and a pair of wings instead?" she muttered.

"I don't have the legs for the cupid look," he said with a grin. When nobody returned it, he shrugged. "Look, I didn't lock you two in. I didn't even realize you were here until security called to let me know that people were locked inside and I realized it must be one or both of you."

A sudden thought smacked her upside the head. Larissa stepped forward, her hands fisting on her hips.

"Was the offer of a storefront a lie? A part of your weird scheme?" The feeling of betrayal was huge. Was this how Jason had felt when he'd thought she cheated on him? And wasn't it ironic that Conner was the center of both their betrayals?

She wanted to pound on something. The bench, the walls, Conner himself.

But down a few layers, beneath her anger and hurt, was a huge sense of relief. Larissa hadn't realized until just this second how glad she'd be to not have her store here. How much she really wanted to stay in the Victorian. With or without the rest of her dream, the Jason and true love forever part of it, she still really wanted the simple joy of owning her own bookstore.

A part of her, the part that'd taken all those business

classes and reworked that damned business plan a million times, was silently screaming "no." No way, she couldn't give up such an incredible opportunity. This was just loser thinking. Her, worrying that she was going to lose out to Jason. Or guilt, since it was so hard to take away a business opportunity from someone she knew really needed it.

"Of course not," Conner said, apparently having taken it upon himself to cause stress and confusion in every aspect of Larissa's life. "The store is available, just like I said. But instead of the committee deciding, I'm leaving it up to the two of you."

"That's crazy," Larissa said, not looking at Jason. After everything she'd admitted already, everything she'd shared, there was no way she was going to tell him that she was having second thoughts. But she definitely didn't want to try to talk him into giving up the store. Especially in light of the fact that she suddenly didn't want it. "How are we supposed to make a decision like that?"

"I don't know. Maybe talk to each other?"

Larissa was about to snap that they'd already tried that. Then she shut her mouth. Because, really, they hadn't. They'd gone down on each other. They'd drove each other crazy. And they'd yelled at each other.

But talk? Not so much.

"We'll figure it out," Jason said, again in that quiet, mellow tone. Larissa half-turned to get a good look at his face, wondering why he wasn't more intense. He met her eyes, giving her a long look that sent her stomach tumbling over itself. So many emotions were there in the blue depths of his gaze.

Confusion was clear. So was desire. She saw a little bit of anger and something else. Something powerful and scary that made her heart race and hope climb way too high for her comfort.

"How are we supposed to figure it out?" she asked, wetting her suddenly dry lips and trying to calm her pounding pulse. She was asking about more than just the store, but wasn't sure if Jason realized that.

"We just need a little time," Jason told her.

Was he seeing into her heart and giving her the answers she most wanted to hear? Or was he obliviously hitting the ones that would only add to her pain later?

"Great," Conner said, his overly jovial tone cutting through the tension. "Then I'll let you two get to it."

He gave them a double thumbs up at odds with his CEO haircut and three-piece suit and skirted around them to head for the front doors.

Larissa and Jason stood silently while he keyed a code into the box on the wall and the bolts slid free of their secure position. Then he twisted the key in the lock. Larissa stepped aside a little so she didn't get mowed down in case Jason decided to rush the door.

"Give me a second to gather my stuff," she said when nobody moved.

"Actually…"

She stopped, her bare feet sliding on the floor as she turned to hear what Conner was going to say. He had a weird look on his face. Similar to the look he'd had yesterday afternoon, just like the look he'd had when he'd confessed to playing matchmaker a few minutes ago.

"Conner…" she warned, hurrying toward him.

"I think you two need to work a few things out," he said as he opened the door.

Before she could reach him, though, he stepped through the doors and quickly slid the key in to lock them from the outside.

"What the hell?"

She ran toward the doors and shook the handle, yelling

over her shoulder to Jason, "Stop him. He's locking us in here again and leaving."

And the sonofabitch did. Larissa cursed, beating her fist on the glass as Conner pocketed the keys and gave her a jaunty little finger wave. Then he glanced at his watch and held up two fingers. She responded by holding up one.

He just laughed and walked away.

Larissa hit the door a couple more times. Then, furious and knowing she'd regret it but unable to stop herself, she kicked the brass plated door with her bare foot. She gave a little scream as pain shot all the way up to her shoulder.

Seething, she spun around. Jason was leaning on the far wall, his arms crossed over his chest. He looked like he was waiting for a freaking bus.

"Why didn't you stop him?" she accused, her fists digging into her hips while she tried to catch her breath.

Jason wasn't winded. Of course, she didn't think he'd moved at all, so that had to factor in. He just stood there against the wall, looking all casual. Had he lost his mind?

"Because I didn't want to."

Oh, yeah. He'd definitely lost his mind.

Knowing she was on her way to looking like the bride of Frankenstein and not caring, Larissa gave her curls a frustrated tug, repeating with each pull, "You. Didn't. Want. To?"

"Nope," he said with a shake of his head. When she stomped over to him, he didn't move, except to arch his brow.

"Why didn't you want to stop him from locking us back in the same miserable state we've just spent the last twelve hours in?" she asked, her voice rising with each word.

"I didn't want to," he said, slowly uncrossing his arms and reaching out to take her hands. "Because I want to fix things with you."

# 14

JASON WASN'T SURE HOW to fix things. He didn't even know exactly what he wanted fixed or in what way. He just knew he didn't want to leave things the way they were.

From the tight look on Larissa's face, maybe she'd have preferred leaving things at their earlier goodbye. He grimaced. Yeah, this pitch was guaranteed to go well.

But what was he pitching for? Now that he stood here, committed to making one last plea, his brain was blank.

"What do you want, Jason? Do you want it all tied up in a tidy bow?" she challenged, the frustration in her voice clear on her face as well. She threw up one hand, narrowly missing his face. "Maybe we can be friends? Or what was it you suggested earlier? Your version of bootie call buddies?"

"Well, you always said I had a fine bootie," he said lightly, more to buy time than because he thought smart-ass comments would earn him a smile.

He was right. He got an eye roll instead. But the tension seemed to drain from Larissa's shoulders and she gave him an indecipherable look before shrugging.

"Look, the only thing we need to fix is this store situation. The rest—" She gave a wave of her hand, whether to dismiss the past or shoo away the present, he wasn't sure. "We said all there is to say about that last night."

"Actually…" He took a deep breath and paused, looking at Larissa. She was gorgeous. Her curls were now a fuzzy halo around her head. The skillfully applied makeup of the previous day was gone, leaving her pale and hollow-eyed. Tension and hurt lingered in her huge dark eyes, and she was wrapped once again in that body-disguising blanket.

Gorgeous.

"Actually," he said again, "I'm not happy with the way we settled things. Not before, and not now."

Her sigh was shaky, nerves playing across her face. She shook her head and gave him a pleading look. "Let's not do this, please? We said things, I said things, that I regret. I shouldn't have compared you to your father. I'm sorry. I really am. But beyond that, I just want to let it go. We need to get out of here and get on with our lives."

It was his turn to shake his head.

"It's not that easy," he told her. Risking everything, he reached out to take her hands in his. He felt her pulse speed through her slender fingers as she tried to tug away, but he held tight. He needed the contact. And if she got mad and tried to take a swing, this should minimize the damage.

"Look," he said quietly, staring into the dark depths of her eyes. "I don't want to let things go. I especially don't want to let you go."

"I beg your pardon?" She pressed her lips together, blinking fast as if trying not to cry. Then she shook her head. "I don't think this is funny, Jason."

"I'm not trying to be funny. I figure Conner did us a favor, bringing us back together like this. And since having an interfering friend create a second chance like this is probably a once-in-a-lifetime thing, we shouldn't waste it."

She gave him a suspicious look. "Seriously, is this another pitch to get me to have sex with you?"

Jason grinned, not so much at her words but at the way she blushed when she said them. They'd spent almost eight hours doing each other every which way, and talking about it still made her cheeks turn pink. God, he loved her.

The realization hit him like a swinging tree branch. Reeling, he sucked in a breath and vowed that this time, he was going to make it work. This time he wasn't going to run away. Not from Larissa, not from commitment, and definitely not from his feelings.

"Not a pitch," he assured her, trying to recapture his smile. "But do me a favor and keep sex between us front and center in your mind."

"Why?"

"Because we're incredible. We're hot and wild and make each other feel things that nobody else can," he insisted. Thrilled that she didn't deny his words, he continued, "We're great together. I've climbed mountains, kayaked oceans and dropped out of planes and none of that comes even close to the thrill I get when I'm making love with you."

Her eyes huge, she took a shaky breath and stared. She reached out, her palm barely grazing his cheek before she pulled back and balled her hand into a fist at her side. Then, her brow knit tight, she shook her head.

"I can't, and won't, deny that the sex is incredible. I feel things with you, do things with you, that I've never imagined with anyone else."

Even though he knew damned well it was inappropriate given the seriousness of their conversation, Jason grinned. Instead of getting mad, Larissa just rolled her eyes. Then she got that serious look again.

"But sex, even mind-blowingly awesome sex, isn't enough," she said quietly.

"It's a start."

"No. When it's all we have between us, it's an end."

He clenched his jaw against the rising panic. He'd never tried to talk someone into a relationship before and the stakes were so high. Dammit, he wished he had time to practice or something.

"No. We have more. We can have as much more as you want," he promised rashly.

"You're just saying that because you want the store," she accused, tears lurking behind the anger in her voice.

Because he wasn't expecting it, this time when she tugged her hands away, she pulled free. Then she took a huge step back, as if putting a big exclamation point at the end of her declaration that she wanted to get away from him.

"You think I'd say all those things, lay myself bare like that, just to get some freaking store?" Fury danced in little black spots before his eyes. Jason couldn't remember ever being this pissed.

How could she make him feel so much love, so much pain and so damned much anger, all at the same time? It shouldn't be possible to feel all of those things at once.

It was too hard. This emotional crap. Romance? Screw this, it demanded too much. He just didn't know if he had that much to give.

And he was asking for more? To sign on to this craziness for the long term? Why was he bothering? Jason started pacing, from one side store to the next then back again, and shoved his hand through his hair. He was crazy. He should have left things alone. He should have stopped Conner from taking off and locking them in again.

He glanced at Larissa, noting how sexy and sweet she looked standing there, all rumpled and mussed. The blanket had slipped off one bare, silky shoulder so he could see the swell of one breast.

He knew she'd be the first to insist that she wasn't looking her best. But he wanted her like crazy. Just looking at her got him hard. Which was saying a lot given that his dick had gotten more loving tonight than it'd had in the last six months combined.

Still, he should have kept his damned pants on.

His hurt must have got through to her like his anger hadn't. Larissa pulled a face, taking step toward him. Not touching, God forbid, but close enough to get in his way.

"I'm not accusing you of lying," she insisted. "I'm just saying that maybe you're so focused on getting the store that you are willing to do anything to make that happen."

"You being anything?"

That took care of the conciliatory light in her eyes. "Are you trying to say you don't want the store?"

"Let's just leave the store out of this for a minute," he demanded, beyond frustrated that he had to explain himself. And that he was doing such an abysmal job of it. No wonder they'd split up before—they clearly had lousy communication skills. "This isn't about the store or either one of our businesses. This is about us. About our future."

"No. There is no us." She shook her head. "And we don't have a future, remember."

"You don't think we should be together?" he asked, working to keep the hurt out of his voice. What the hell had he been thinking? He'd had it right before, to keep most of his heart tucked away safe and hidden instead of putting himself out there and believing they could have a real relationship.

"I don't think we *can* be together," she said with a sniff, the tears in her eyes finally pooling over and starting to run down her cheeks.

"Fine." His heart ached, but he'd be damned if he was

going to beg. Jason started to turn away, then gave a frustrated growl and stopped.

He couldn't just give up. Instead, he gave her a long, intense inspection. Pain and regret were clear on her face. But as he looked closer, he saw resignation. She expected him to walk away. She knew if she pushed, he'd just toss up his hands and go. And he'd damn near proved her right.

"Look, I know we blew it before," he paused, waiting to see if she still thought the blowing was all his doing. When she just sighed, her shoulders sagging a little, he continued, "But I'm not giving up this time."

He reached for her hands again, pulling her closer.

"You're not ready to trust me, that's fine. Eventually you will. I'm sticking around this time," he decided.

As he said the words, it was like a light went off in his heart. It didn't matter if she believed him, or if she was ready. He was willing to do whatever it took to make things work between them. He was sticking it out. He was through running. It might be tomorrow or it might be a year from now. Sooner or later, she'd realize they would make it.

"Sticking around?" Skepticism coated her words.

"Yeah. I can't cut back my trips since I've got financial responsibilities I can't shirk, but no more personal trips unless you want to go with me. Maybe places like Barbados or Greece? Those are romantic, right?"

She stared. Her lips opened but no words came out.

"I'm still bunking at my parents' house, but Peter and Meghan are going to live there after they get married. I'll get an apartment instead of taking their spare room. Or maybe I'll even put a down payment on a house," he mused. Now that he was fixating on this settling down thing, it was feeling like its own adventure. One he planned to spend with Larissa.

"You're seriously thinking about buying a house?" Her

tone said she thought the only thing he was serious about was bullshitting her.

"Yeah," he decided. He remembered something she'd said one night years ago, curled up in his arms after they'd made love. "Maybe one of those Victorian houses like Murphy's store? You dig those, right? Didn't you say that's the kind of place you'd like to buy someday? Once the bookstore is gone, you'll be missing that old-house vibe. So until you believe I'm serious, you can come hang at my place and get your old-house thrills."

She pulled away. Again. He was starting to think she should be wearing a cord, she was in and out of his arms like a yo-yo.

Three feet away, she started pacing. Every few steps she shot him a confused look. Jason just waited.

"And if I say I want to keep the store?" she finally asked.

He grimaced. He wanted to tell her he'd step aside. He wanted to promise her anything. But this wasn't just about his wants.

"Maybe we can go get some coffee, real food and talk about it? If you can help me figure out a way to keep things going so I can still cover my mom's care until Peter starts bringing in enough to really help out, then I'll step aside."

The waiting, and the stepping aside to let her decide, were about the hardest things Jason had ever done. God, why hadn't he just handed over the store? Why hadn't he promised her anything, everything, to get her to agree to get back together with him? Knowing he'd just blown all his romance points, Jason mentally cringed, waiting for her to tell him to get screwed.

Instead, she gave a long, shuddering breath and closed her eyes for a second. When she opened them, she looked so peaceful and happy he knew this was the kiss-off.

"You can have the store," she said.

"What?" he exclaimed, sure he'd heard her wrong. "Why?"

"Because…" She hesitated, then shrugged and said quietly, "Because I love you."

LARISSA WAITED FOR THE ROOF to cave in. Or for Jason's eyes to bug out like a cartoon character's right before he left a body-shaped hole in the wall when he ran away.

But he didn't run. He just grinned like he'd just been handed a check for a million dollars. By a naked woman. Dangling the keys to a Lamborghini on her equally naked finger.

"Look, I definitely want you to keep loving me," he said, his grin widening again as he said the words. "But I don't want you making any sacrifices for me. For us."

He made a c'mere wiggle with his fingers, obviously preferring that this conversation take place in his arms.

Larissa stepped backward instead. She preferred this conversation take place with all her brain cells intact.

"What about a compromise?" she offered, hoping she was making the right decision here. She had this big huge dream at her fingertips yet she was thinking about tossing it aside for a more comfortable, non-fancy dream. How was Jason going to think she was amazing and special if she settled?

How could she compete with his exciting life if she was, well, not exciting?

His grin turned into a frown when she wouldn't let him hug her. "What kind of compromise?"

"You take the store, but help me make my romance column a little sexier," she said through a tight throat as her stomach churned with nerves. Was that enough? She knew it would be for her, but what about him? "I'm realizing that romance is definitely better with a little heat."

"That will be my pleasure," he promised. "But what about

your business? I thought this mall was perfect for your plans. Are you sure you're okay with giving it up?"

"I'm sure. If I realized one thing being trapped in here, it was that I don't quite fit. I'd never be comfortable, never feel like I could be myself in this place." She waited to see if he was going to lecture her, but he just gave the fancy store signs a sneer.

"Besides," she continued, "the real benefit that makes this location pay off is the promotion. And that's something you could use much more than I could."

"I thought you wanted your store here? Didn't you say this was the perfect place to showcase Isn't It Romantic's message?"

She stared down the length of the mall, noting the fancy store names and the feeling they invoked. Definitely not a feeling of welcome, or of love. Even if she was sure she'd get a little hot and excited whenever she saw them again, given how wild the lovemaking had gotten between her and Jason.

"This place is too superficial for romance." Finally sure, and ready, she stepped forward and laid her palm against Jason's chest, so warm and hard beneath his shirt. "Isn't It Romantic wouldn't fit. I let my self-doubts and insecurities fog my judgment."

"But what are you going to do?" he asked as he lay his own hand over hers while wrapping his other one around her waist and pulling her closer.

"I'm going to buy out Mr. Murphy and turn the book-store into my dream store." Just saying the words sent a thrill of rightness through her. It fit her, just like Jason did. "I've always wanted the store. And like you said, I love the Victorian. I'll shift it from books to my romance niche and it'll be perfect."

"I thought you were worried about the location?"

She grimaced. Since when was Jason the harbinger of reality? "I am, a little. But I'll figure something out."

"How about we setup a little display in the store here? Feature the adventurous side of romance?"

"That's perfect," she said with a relieved smile. "Are you sure Peter won't mind? He'll be taking the job of running your place here, right?"

"No. Actually, that job will be both of ours. If Peter wants to make this work, he's going to have to take turns."

"Take turns?" Larissa reached up, her fingers reveling in the soft, silky feel of his hair as she brushed the lock off his forehead. "You mean take turns going off and having adventures?"

Jason caught her hand and brought her fingers to his mouth, brushing his lips over them before pressing a damp kiss to her palm. Larissa shivered as desire heated low in her belly. For a brief second, she wished the power—especially the power running the video cameras—was out again so they could have a little privacy to explore the sensual heat warming her girly parts.

"No. Take turns staying home with the women we love."

Larissa's mind, so busy entertaining the image of dragging him into the store's bathroom with all its privacy for some fast and hot sex, went blank.

"You love me?" she asked, both exhilarated and terrified. "Really, this time?"

"I love you," he confirmed, pressing her hand to his chest. His eyes held hers captive as he leaned down, saying just before he took her mouth, "Really, this time."

Their lips slid together in a soft, sweet promise that brought more tears to Larissa's eyes. Then, as if realizing sentiment was going to ruin their hot moment, Jason deepened the kiss. His tongue begged entrance, then proceeded to drive her crazy. Twining, dancing, entrancing, he held her mouth captive as he curved his fingers into her hair and lifted her mouth to more perfectly fit against his.

"Maybe we should send Conner a thank-you gift," she teased as they ended the kiss, her fingers twining through the hair at the nape of his neck. "You know, to show our appreciation for his trapping us together here."

Jason laughed, then glanced down the length of the mall and got a wicked look in his eyes.

"I've got just the thing."

She followed his gaze, seeing the bench they'd had their lousy meal on. She frowned, then spied the long box tucked underneath it.

"You'd give him your dick?" she said with a laugh.

"Not my dick," he corrected after a quick wince. He gripped her hips and pulled her closer to make sure she knew his was still there, hard and happy. "But I'll give him the koteka. We've already enjoyed its special powers so it's only fair to pass it on. And I think he'd get a kick out of it."

"You don't want to save that for your museum?" she asked, twining her arms around his neck and nuzzling his throat.

"The only big person I want seeing my big woody is you," he teased, his arms banding tight around her like he didn't ever want to let go. Then his tone turned serious and he said, "But this is about more than sex, okay? I'm not looking for that bootie call. I'm looking for a real relationship. One where we trust each other and depend on each other and all that grown up romance stuff."

Laughing, she nodded. Before she could say anything, he continued, "I don't want to date. Or to live together. I don't even want to get engaged. I want to move right past go and get married."

Married?

Holy shit. Larissa could see how serious he was. There was no hesitation in his eyes, no worry or doubt. Instead she saw only love and confidence.

As joy and excitement fought for top emotional billing, Larissa leaned back, wondering how she'd gotten so lucky. But fear still lingered.

"You're sure?" she asked quietly. "I mean, this time I have expectations. Real ones. A lifetime of them."

His smile was slow, sweet and positive. He nodded, then wrapping his hands tighter around her waist to lift her to her tiptoes, he brushed a soft kiss over her lips.

"I'm sure enough for a lifetime," he promised. "I believe in us, Larissa. I believe that I'm the man to make you happy. And I believe you're the woman I want to spend my forever with."

She gave a tremulous smile and, finally believing it was for real, nodded. "Then yes. I want to marry you. I want to spend my life with you. Build our careers and hold each other's hands as we face whatever comes our way."

He laid his forehead against hers and closed his eyes, giving a huge sigh of relief. Then he opened his eyes, brushed another soft kiss over her lips and arched his brow.

"You're sure? Because there's no backing out or easy misunderstandings this time. If we do this, it's for the long haul."

Larissa stared at his gorgeous face, the hope and love shining from his blue eyes. How could she ever have doubted that he was her perfect romance hero?

"Yes. I'm ready for the long haul," she vowed.

His laughter bounced off the walls as he swept her into his arms and started heading down the mall. Larissa wrapped her hands around his neck to hold on, laughing along with him. "Where are we going?" she asked.

"Conner said two hours. We have one left and I'm planning to make good use of it."

"More gratuitous sex?" she teased.

"More like grateful, amazing sex," he corrected, pausing in the doorway of the store to kiss her.

As his lips slid over hers, Larissa had to agree.

She was very, very grateful, and the sex between them? Definitely amazing.

\* \* \* \* \*

# COMING NEXT MONTH

## Available May 31, 2011

**#615 REAL MEN WEAR PLAID!**
*Encounters*
Rhonda Nelson

**#616 TERMS OF SURRENDER**
*Uniformly Hot!*
Leslie Kelly

**#617 RECKLESS PLEASURES**
*The Pleasure Seekers*
Tori Carrington

**#618 SHOULD'VE BEEN A COWBOY**
*Sons of Chance*
Vicki Lewis Thompson

**#619 HOT TO THE TOUCH**
*Checking E-Males*
Isabel Sharpe

**#620 MINE UNTIL MORNING**
*24 Hours: Blackout*
Samantha Hunter

> You can find more information on upcoming
> Harlequin® titles, free excerpts and more at
> **www.HarlequinInsideRomance.com.**

HBCNM0511

# REQUEST YOUR FREE BOOKS!
## 2 FREE NOVELS PLUS 2 FREE GIFTS!

### red-hot reads!

"Thanks for not turning on the lights," Tyler said. "I'm a mess."

"Not in my book." Even in low light, Alex had a good view of her yellow shirt plastered to her body. It was all he could do not to reach for her, mud and all. But the next move needed to be hers, not his.

She slicked her wet hair back and squeezed some water out of the ends as she glanced upward. "I like the sound of the rain on a tin roof."

"Me, too."

She met his gaze briefly and looked away. "Where's the sink?"

"At the far end, beyond the last stall."

Tyler's running shoes squished as she walked down the aisle between the rows of stalls. She glanced sideways at Alex. "So how much of a cowboy are you these days? Do you ride the range and stuff?"

"I ride." He liked being able to say that. "Why?"

"Just wondered. Last summer, you were still a city boy. You even told me you weren't the cowboy type, but you're…different now."

He wasn't sure if that was a good thing or a bad thing. Maybe she preferred city boys to cowboys. "How am I different?"

"Well, you dress differently, and your hair's a little longer. Your face seems a little more chiseled, but maybe that's because of your hair. Also, there's something else, something harder to define, an attitude…"

"Are you saying I have an attitude?"

"Not in a bad way. It's more like a quiet confidence."

He was flattered, but still he had to laugh. "I just admitted a while ago that I have all kinds of doubts about this event tomorrow. That doesn't seem like quiet confidence to me."

"This isn't about your job, it's about…your…" She took a deep breath. "It's about your sex appeal, okay? I have no business talking about it, because it will only make me want to do things I shouldn't do." She started toward the end of the barn. "Now, where's that sink? We need to get cleaned up and go back to the house. Dinner is probably ready, and I—"

He spun her around and pulled her into his arms, mud and all. "Let's do those things." Then he kissed her, knowing that she would kiss him back, knowing that this time he would take that kiss where he wanted it to go. And she would let him.

*Follow Tyler and Alex's wild adventures in*
*SHOULD'VE BEEN A COWBOY*
*Available June 2011 only from Harlequin® Blaze™*
*wherever books are sold.*